'What is the p[...]
pleasure?'

'Neither.'

'I'm sorry?' She was a pear-shaped, slug-coloured, short-haired woman wearing big glasses and a dark blue uniform.

'I'm here to collect my father's corpse,' mumbled Patrick.

'I'm sorry, sir, I didn't catch that,' she said with official exasperation.

'I'm here to collect my father's corpse,' Patrick shouted slowly.

She handed back his passport. 'Have a nice day.'

Edward St. Aubyn was born in 1960. He has written for the *Spectator*, the *Times Literary Supplement*, *Tatler*, *Books & Bookmen* and Radio 3's *New Premisses*. *Bad News* is his second novel. His first, *Never Mind*, was published in February 1992, and won a Betty Trask Award.

Also by Edward St. Aubyn

Never Mind

Edward St. Aubyn

BAD NEWS

Mandarin

A Mandarin Paperback
BAD NEWS

First published in Great Britain 1992
by William Heinemann Ltd
This edition published 1994
by Mandarin Paperbacks
an imprint of Reed Consumer Books Ltd
Michelin House, 81 Fulham Road, London SW3 6RB
and Auckland, Melbourne, Singapore and Toronto

Copyright © Edward St. Aubyn 1992
The author has asserted his moral rights

A CIP catalogue record for this title
is available from the British Library
ISBN 0 7493 1654 3

Printed and bound in Great Britain
by Cox & Wyman Ltd, Reading, Berkshire

For Dee

CHAPTER ONE

Patrick pretended to sleep, hoping the seat next to him would remain empty, but he soon heard a brief-case sliding into the overhead compartment. Opening his eyes reluctantly, he saw a tall snub-nosed man.

'Hi, I'm Earl Hammer,' said the man, extending a big freckled hand covered in thick blond hair, 'I guess I'm your seating companion.'

'Patrick Melrose,' said Patrick mechanically, offering a clammy and slightly shaking hand to Mr Hammer.

Early the previous evening, George Watford had telephoned Patrick from New York.

'Patrick, my dear,' he said in a strained and drawling voice, slightly delayed by its Atlantic crossing, 'I'm afraid I have the most awful news for you: your father died the night before last in his hotel room. I've been quite unable to get hold of either you or your mother – I believe she's in Chad with the Save the Children Fund – but I need hardly tell you how I feel; I adored your father, as you know. Oddly enough, he was supposed to be having lunch with me at the Key Club on the day that he died, but of course he never turned up; I remember thinking how unlike him it was. It must be the most awful shock for you. Everybody liked him, you know, Patrick. I've told some of the members there and some of the servants, and they were *very* sorry to hear about his death.'

'Where is he now?' asked Patrick coldly.

'At Frank E. MacDonald's in Madison Avenue. It's the place everyone uses over here, I believe it's awfully good.'

Patrick promised that as soon as he arrived in New York he would call George.

'I'm sorry to be the bringer of such bad news,' said George. 'You're going to need all your courage during this difficult time.'

'Thanks for calling,' said Patrick, 'I'll see you tomorrow.'

'Goodbye, my dear.'

Patrick put down the syringe he had been flushing out, and sat beside the phone without moving. Was it bad news? Perhaps he would need all his courage not to dance in the street, not to smile too broadly. Sunlight poured in through the blurred and caked window-panes of his flat. Outside, in Ennismore Gardens, the leaves of the plane trees were painfully bright.

2

He suddenly leaped out of his chair. 'You're not going to get away with this,' he muttered vindictively. The sleeve of his shirt rolled forward and absorbed the trickle of blood on his arm.

'You know, Paddy,' said Earl, regardless of the fact that nobody called Patrick 'Paddy', 'I've made a hell of a lot of money, and I figured it was time to enjoy some of the good things in life.'

It was half an hour into the flight and Paddy was already Earl's good buddy.

'How sensible of you,' gasped Patrick.

'I've rented an apartment by the beach in Monte Carlo, and a house in the hills behind Monaco. *Just a beautiful house*,' said Earl, shaking his head incredulously. 'I've got an English butler: he tells me what sports jacket to wear – can you believe that? And I've got the leisure time to read the *Wall Street Journal* from cover to cover.'

'A heady freedom,' said Patrick.

'It's *great*. And I'm also reading a real interesting book at the moment, called *Megatrends*. *And* a Chinese classic on the art of war. Are you interested in war at all?'

'Not madly,' said Patrick.

'I guess I'm biased: I was in Vietnam,' said Earl, staring at the horizon through the tiny window of the plane.

'You liked it?'

3

'Sure did,' Earl smiled.

'Didn't you have any reservations?'

'I'll tell you, Paddy, the only reservations I had about Vietnam were the target restrictions. Flying over some of those ports and seeing tankers deliver oil you *knew* was for the Viet Cong, and not being able to strike them – that was one of the most frustrating experiences of my life.' Earl, who seemed to be in an almost perpetual state of amazement at the things he said, shook his head again.

Patrick turned towards the aisle, suddenly assailed by the sound of his father's music, as clear and loud as breaking glass, but this aural hallucination was soon swamped by the vitality of his neighbour.

'Have you ever been to the Tahiti Club in St Tropez, Paddy? That's a hell of a place! I met a couple of dancers there,' his voice dropped half an octave to match the new tone of male camaraderie, 'I got to tell you,' he said confidentially, 'I love to screw. God, I *love* it,' he shouted. 'But a great body is not enough, you know what I mean? You gotta have that *mental thing*. I was screwing these two dancers: they were *fantastic* women, great bodies, just beautiful, but I couldn't come. You know why?'

'You didn't have that mental thing,' suggested Patrick.

'That's right! I didn't have that *mental thing*,' said Earl.

* * *

Perhaps it was that mental thing that was missing with Debbie. He had called her last night to tell her about his father's death.

'Oh, God, that's appalling,' she stammered, 'I'll come over straight away.'

Patrick could hear the nervous tension in Debbie's voice, the inherited anxiety about the correct thing to say. With parents like hers, it was not surprising that embarrassment had become the strongest emotion in her life. Debbie's father, an Australian painter called Peter Hickmann, was a notorious bore. Patrick once heard him introduce an anecdote with the words, 'That reminds me of my best bouillabaisse story'. Half an hour later, Patrick could only count himself lucky that he was not listening to Peter's second best bouillabaisse story.

Debbie's mother, whose neurotic resources made her resemble a battery-operated stick insect, had social ambitions which were not in her power to fulfil while Peter stood at her side telling his bouillabaisse stories. A well-known professional party planner, she was foolish enough to take her own advice. The brittle perfection of her entertainments turned to dust when human beings were introduced into the airless arena of her drawing room. Like a mountaineer expiring at base camp, she passed on her boots to Debbie, and with them the awesome responsibility: *to climb*. Mrs Hickmann was inclined to forgive Patrick the apparent purposelessness of his life and the sinister pallor of his complexion, when she considered that he had an income of one hundred thousand pounds a year, and came from a family which, although it had done nothing since, had seen the Norman invasion from the winning side. It was not perfect, but it would do. After all, Patrick was only twenty-two.

Meanwhile, Peter continued to weave life into anecdote and to describe grand incidents in his daughter's life to the fast-emptying bar of the Travellers' Club where, after forty years of stiff opposition, he had been elected in a moment of weakness which all the members who had since been irradiated by his conversation bitterly regretted.

After Patrick had discouraged Debbie from coming round to see him, he set out for a walk through Hyde Park, tears stinging his eyes. It was a hot dry evening, full of pollen and dust. Sweat trickled down his ribs and broke out on his forehead. Over the Serpentine, a wisp of cloud dissolved in front of the sun, which sank, swollen and red, through a bruise of pollution. On the scintillating water yellow and blue boats bobbed up and down. Patrick stood still and watched a police car drive very fast along the path behind the boathouses. He vowed he would take no more heroin. This was the most important moment in his life and he must get it right. He had to get it right.

Patrick lit a Turkish cigarette and asked the stewardess for another glass of brandy. He was beginning to feel a little jumpy without any smack. The four valiums he had stolen from Kay had helped him face breakfast, but now he could feel the onset of withdrawal, like a litter of drowning kittens in the sack of his stomach.

Kay was the American girl he had been having an affair with. Last night when he had wanted to bury himself in a woman's body, to affirm that, unlike his father, he was alive, he had chosen to see Kay. Debbie was beautiful (everybody said so), and she was clever (she said so herself), but he could imagine her clicking anxiously across the room, like a pair of chopsticks, and just then he needed a softer embrace.

Kay lived in a rented flat on the outskirts of Oxford, where she played the violin, kept cats, and worked on her Kafka thesis. She took a less complacent attitude towards Patrick's idleness than anyone else he knew. 'You have to sell yourself,' she used to say, 'just to get rid of the damned thing.'

Patrick disliked everything about Kay's flat. He knew she had not put the gold cherubs against the William Morris-styled wallpaper; on the other hand, she had not taken them down. In the dark corridor, Kay had come up to him, her thick brown hair falling on one shoulder, and her body draped in heavy grey silk. She had kissed him slowly, while her jealous cats scratched at the kitchen door.

Patrick had drunk the whisky and taken the valium she had given him. Kay told him about her own dying parents. 'You have to start looking after them badly before you've got over the shock of how badly they looked after you,' she said. 'I had to drive my parents across the States last summer. My dad was dying of emphysema and my mother, who used to be a ferocious woman, was like a child after her stroke. I was barreling along at eighty through Utah, looking for a bottle of oxygen, while my mother kept saying with her impoverished vocabulary, "Oh dear, Oh my, Papa's not well. Oh my."'

Patrick imagined Kay's father sunk in the back of the car, his eyes glazed over with exhaustion and his lungs, like torn fishing nets, trawling vainly for air. How had his own father died? He had forgotten to ask.

Since his luminous remarks about 'that mental thing', Earl had been speaking about his 'wide variety of holdings' and his love for his family. His divorce had been 'hard on the kids', but he concluded with a chuckle, 'I've been diversifying, and I don't just mean in the business field.'

Patrick was grateful to be flying on Concorde. Not only would he be fresh for the ordeal of seeing his father's corpse, before it was cremated the next day, but he was also halving his conversation time with Earl. They ought to advertise. A simpering voice-over popped into his mind: 'It's because we care, not just for your physical comfort, but for your mental

8

health, that we shorten your conversation with people like Earl Hammer.'

'You see, Paddy,' said Earl, 'I've made very considerable – I mean *big* – contributions to the Republican party, and I could get just about any embassy I want. But I'm not interested in London or Paris: that's just social shit.'

Patrick drank his brandy in one gulp.

'What I want is a small Latin American or Central American country where the ambassador has control of the C.I.A. *on the ground*.'

'On the ground,' echoed Patrick.

'That's right,' said Earl. 'But I have a dilemma at this point; a real hard one.' He was solemn again. 'My daughter is trying to make the national volley ball team and she has a series of real important games over the next year. Hell, I don't know whether to go for the embassy or root for my daughter.'

'Earl,' said Patrick earnestly, 'I don't think there's anything more important than being a good dad.'

Earl was visibly moved. 'I appreciate that advice, Paddy, I really do.'

The flight was coming to an end. Earl made some remarks about how you always met 'high quality' people on Concorde. At the airport terminal Earl took the US citizens channel, and Patrick headed for the Aliens.

'Goodbye, friend,' shouted Earl with a big wave, 'see you around!'

'Every parting,' snarled Patrick under his breath, 'is a little death.'

CHAPTER TWO

'What is the purpose of your visit, sir? Business or pleasure?'

'Neither.'

'I'm sorry?' She was a pear-shaped, slug-coloured, short-haired woman wearing big glasses and a dark blue uniform.

'I'm here to collect my father's corpse,' mumbled Patrick.

'I'm sorry, sir, I didn't catch that,' she said with official exasperation.

'*I'm here to collect my father's corpse,*' Patrick shouted slowly.

She handed back his passport. 'Have a nice day.'

The rage that Patrick had felt after passing through passport control eclipsed his usual terror of Customs (what if they stripped him? What if they saw his arms?).

And so here he was again, slumped in the back of a cab, in a seat often-repaired with black masking tape, but still opening occasionally onto small craters of yellow foam, back in a nation that was dieting its way to immortality, while he still dieted his way in the opposite direction.

As his taxi bounced and squeaked along the freeway, Patrick started to register reluctantly the sensations of re-entry into New York. There was of course a driver who spoke no English, and whose lugubrious photograph confirmed the suicidal gloom which the back of his neck could only hint at. The neighbouring lanes bore witness to the usual combination of excess and decay. Enormous battered cars with sloppy engines, and black-windowed limos, swarmed into the city, like flies on their favourite food. Patrick stared at the dented hubcap of an old white stationwagon. It had seen so much, he reflected, and remembered nothing, like a slick amnesiac reeling in thousands of images and rejecting them instantly, spinning out its empty life under a paler wider sky.

The thought that had obsessed him the night before cut into his trance. It was intolerable: his father had cheated him again. The bastard had deprived him of the chance to transform his ancient terror and his unwilling admiration into contemptuous pity for the boring and toothless old man he had become. And yet Patrick found himself sucked towards his father's death by a stronger habit of emulation than he could reasonably bear. Death was always, of course, a *temptation*; but now it seemed like a temptation to obey. On top of its power to strike a decadent or defiant posture in the endless vaudeville of youth, on top of the familiar lure of raw violence and self-destruction, it had taken on the aspect of conformity, like going into the family business. Really, it had all the options covered.

Acre after acre of tombstones stretched out beside the freeway. Patrick thought of his favourite lines of poetry: 'Dead, long dead, / Long dead!' (how could you beat that?) 'And my heart is a handful of dust, / And the wheels go over my head, / And my bones are shaken with pain, / For into a shallow grave they are thrust, / Only a yard beneath the street,' something, something, 'enough to drive one mad'.

The slippery humming metal of the Williamsburg Bridge reawakened him to his surroundings, but not for long. He felt queasy and nervous. Another withdrawal in a foreign hotel room; he knew the routine. Except that this was going to be the last time. Or *among* the last times. He laughed nervously. No the bastards weren't going to get him. Concentration like a flame-thrower. No prisoners!

The trouble was that he always wanted smack, like wanting to get out of a wheelchair when the room was on fire. If you thought about it that much you might as well take it. His right leg twitched up and down rapidly. He folded his arms across his stomach and pinched the collar of his overcoat together. 'Fuck off,' he said out loud, 'just fuck off.'

Into the gorgeous streets. Blocks of light and shadow. Down the avenue, lights turning green all the way. Light and shadow, ticking like a metronome, as they surged over the curve of the earth under a paler wider sky.

It was late May, it was hot, and he really ought to take off his overcoat, but his overcoat was his defence against the thin shards of glass that passers-by slipped casually under his skin, not to mention the slow-motion explosion of shop windows, the bone-rattling thunder of subway trains, and the heartbreaking passage of each second, like a grain of sand trickling through the hourglass of his body. No, he would not take off his overcoat. Do you ask a lobster to disrobe?

He glanced up and saw that he was on Sixth Avenue. Forty-Second Street, Forty-Third Street, row after Mies van der Rohe. Who had said that? He couldn't remember. Other people's words drifted through his mind, like the tumble weed across a windy desert in the opening shots of *They Came from Outer Space*.

And what about all the characters who inhabited him, as if he was a cheap hotel: Gift o' the Gab O'Connor and The Fat Man, and Mrs Garsington, and all the rest of them, longing to push him aside and have their say. Sometimes he felt like a television on which somebody else was changing the channels impatiently and very fast. Well, they could just fuck off as well. This time he was going to fall apart *silently*.

They were getting near the Pierre now. The land of the static electric shock. Doorknobs and lift buttons spitting sparks at a body which had generated its way through miles of thick carpet before forgetting to earth itself. It was here that he had begun his delirious decline on his last visit to New York. From a suite with as much *chinoiserie* as a person could be expected to take, and a view on the Park from far above the cry of traffic, he had slipped down, via the world-famous seediness of the Chelsea Hotel, and landed in a coffin-sized room at the bottom of a garbage-filled well-shaft on Eighth Street, between C and D. From this vantage he had looked back with nostalgia on the hotel he had despised only a few weeks earlier for having a rat in its fridge.

Still, throughout this decline in his accommodation, Patrick had never spent less than five thousand dollars a week on heroin and cocaine. Ninety per cent of the drugs were for him and ten per cent for Natasha, a woman who remained an impenetrable mystery to him during the six months they lived together. The only thing he felt certain about was that she irritated him; but then, who didn't? He continually longed for an uncontaminated solitude, and when he got it he longed for it to stop.

'Hotel,' said the driver.

'About fucking time,' mumbled Patrick.

A grey-coated doorman lifted his cap and held out his hand, while a bellboy hurried out to fetch Patrick's bags. One welcome and two tips later Patrick was stalking sweatily through the long corridor which led to the reception. The tables in the Oval Room were occupied by pairs of lunching women, toying with plates of different-coloured lettuces and ignoring glasses of mineral water. Patrick caught sight of himself in a large gilt mirror, and noticed that, as usual, he looked rather overdressed and extremely ill. There was a disturbing contrast between the care with which the clothes had been assembled, and the ease with which the face looked as if it might fall apart. His very long black overcoat, dark blue suit and thin black and silver tie (bought by his father in the early sixties) seemed to be unrelated to the chaotic tangle of brown hair which surrounded his dead-white and shiny face. The face itself was in a spasm of contradiction. The full lips were pinched inwards, the eyes reduced to narrow slits the nose, which was permanently blocked, forced him to breathe through his open mouth and made him look rather imbecilic; and a frown concentrated his forehead into a vertical crease directly above the nose.

After he had registered, Patrick braced himself to clear as quickly as possible the long gauntlet of welcomes and tips that still lay between him and having a drink in his room. Someone took him to the lift, someone took him up in the lift (that long stale suspense, watching the numbers flicker up to 39), someone showed him how to turn on the television, someone put his suitcase down on the rack, someone pointed out the bathroom light, someone gave him his room key, and, at last, someone brought him a bottle of Jack Daniel's and a black bucket of frail ice cubes, and four glasses.

16

He poured himself a full glass over a few cubes of ice. The smell of the bourbon seemed to him infinitely subtle and poignant, and as he gulped down the first burning mouthful, standing by the window, looking out over Central Park, leafy and hot under a paler wider sky, he wanted to cry. It was so fucking beautiful. He felt his sadness and exhaustion fuse with the dissolving and sentimental embrace of the bourbon. It was a moment of catastrophic charm. How could he ever hope to give up drugs? They filled him with such intense emotion. The sense of power they gave him was, admittedly, rather subjective (ruling the world from under the bedcovers, until the milkman arrived and you thought he was a platoon of stormtroopers come to steal your drugs and splatter your brains across the wall), but then again, *life* was so subjective.

He really ought to go to the funeral parlour now, it would be appalling to miss the chance of seeing his father's corpse (perhaps he could rest his foot on it). Patrick giggled and put down his empty glass on the window-sill. He was not going to take any smack. 'I want to make that *absolutely* clear,' he squealed in the voice of Mr Muffet, his old chemistry teacher from school. Walk tall, that was his philosophy, *but get some downers first*. Nobody could give up everything at once, especially (sob, sob) at a time like this. He must go down into that pulsing, burgeoning, monstrous mass of vegetation, the Park, and score.

The gaggle of black and Hispanic dealers who hung

around the entrance to Central Park opposite his hotel recognised Patrick as a potential customer from some way off.

'Uppers! Downers! Check it out,' said a tall, bruised-looking black man. Patrick walked on.

A hollow-cheeked Hispanic with a scrawny beard jerked his jaw forward and said, 'Wot canna du for ju, my friend?'

'I got goo-ood stuff,' said another black man, wearing shades. '*Check it out.*'

'Have you got any Quaaludes?' drawled Patrick.

'Sure, I got some Quaaludes. I got Lemon 714s – how many you want?'

'How much?'

'Five dollars.'

'I'll take six. And maybe some speed,' Patrick added. This was what they called impulse shopping. Speed was the last thing he wanted, but he didn't like to buy a drug unless he had the capacity to contradict it.

'I got some Beauties, they're Phar-ma-ceu-tical.'

'You mean you made them yourself.'

'No, man, pharmaceutical mean they're goo-ood shit.'

'Three of those.'

'Ten dollars each.'

Patrick handed over sixty dollars and took the pills.

By this time the other dealers had gathered round, impressed by the easy way that Patrick parted with money.

'Ju English, right?' said the Hispanic.

'Don't bother the man,' said Shades.

'Yes,' said Patrick, knowing what was coming next.

'You got free heroin over there, right?' said the bruised-looking black man.

'That's right,' said Patrick patriotically.

'One day I'm going to come over to Britain and get me some of that free smack,' the bruised-looking man said, looking relieved for a few seconds.

'You do that,' said Patrick, heading back up the steps to Fifth Avenue. 'Bye now.'

'You come back here tomorrow,' said Shades possessively.

'Yeah,' mumbled Patrick, running up the steps.

He put the Quaalude in his mouth, summoned a little saliva, and managed to force the pill down. It was an important skill to be able to swallow a pill without anything to drink. People who needed a drink were intolerable, he reflected, hailing a cab.

'Madison Avenue and Eighty-second Street,' he said, realising that the Quaalude, which was after all a large pill, was stuck half-way down his throat. As the cab sped up Madison Avenue, Patrick, twisted his neck into various positions in an attempt to get the pill all the way down.

By the time they reached Frank E. MacDonald's Patrick was stretched out with his neck craned backwards and sideways over the edge of the seat, his hair touching the black rubber floormat while he squeezed as much saliva as he could from the sides of his dry cheeks and swallowed furiously. The driver looked in the rear-view mirror. Another weirdo.

Patrick eventually dislodged the Quaalude from the ledge it had found just under his Adam's apple, and walked through the tall oak doors of the funeral parlour, dread and absurdity competing inside him. The young woman behind the curved oak counter with Doric half-columns set at either end of its inner panel wore a blue jacket and a grey silk blouse, like an air hostess for a flight into the Afterlife.

'I've come to see the corpse of David Melrose,' said Patrick coldly. She told him to step right into the elevator and go 'straight on up' to the third floor, as if he might be tempted to stop off and see some other corpses on the way.

The lift was a homage to French tapestry-making. Above the buttoned leather bench, on which the bereaved could pause before facing the corpse of their loved one, was an Arcadia of *petit point* where a courtier pretending to be a shepherd played a flute to a courtier pretending to be a shepherdess.

This was it, the big moment: the corpse of his chief enemy, the ruins of his creator, the body of his dead father; the great weight of all that was unsaid and would never have been said; the pressure to say it now, when there was nobody to hear, and to speak also on his father's behalf, in an act of self-division that might fissure the world and turn his body into a jigsaw puzzle. *This was it*.

The sound that greeted Patrick as the doors of the lift slid open made him wonder if George had organised a surprise party, but the idea was too grotesque, given the difficulty of procuring more than half a dozen people *worldwide* who knew his father at all well and still liked him. He stepped out onto the landing and saw, beyond two Corinthian pillars, a panelled room full of gaily dressed elderly strangers. Men in every variety of light-weight tartan, and women in big white and yellow hats, were drinking cocktails and clutching each other's arms. At the back of the room, into which he wandered uncomprehendingly, was an open tilted coffin lined with white satin, and containing a punctiliously dressed, diminutive man with a diamond tie-pin, snow-white hair and a black suit. On a table beside him Patrick saw a stack of cards saying, 'In Loving Memory of Hermann Newton'. Death was no doubt an overwhelming experience, but it must be even more powerful than he had imagined if it could transform his father into a small Jew with so many amusing new friends.

Patrick's heart thudded into action. He spun round and stormed back to the lift, where he received a static electric shock when he pushed the call button. 'I can't fucking believe it,' he snarled, kicking a Louis XV-styled chair. The lift doors opened to reveal a fat old man with sagging grey flesh, wearing a pair of extraordinary Bermuda shorts and a yellow T-shirt. Hermann had obviously left a No Mourning clause in his will. Or maybe people were just happy to see him dead, thought Patrick. Beside the fat man stood his blowsy wife, also in beachwear, and next to her was the young woman from the reception desk.

'Wrong fucking corpse,' said Patrick, glaring at her.

'Oh, ho. Whoa there,' said the fat man, as if Patrick was overstating his case.

'Try again,' said Patrick, ignoring the old couple as they waddled past.

He gave the receptionist his special melt-down-and-die stare, with eyebeams as heavy as scaffolding shooting across the space between them and pouring radioactivity into her brain. She seemed unperturbed.

'I'm certain we don't have another party in the building at the moment,' she said.

'I don't want to go to a party,' said Patrick. 'I want to see my father.'

When they had reached the ground floor, the receptionist walked over to the counter where Patrick had first seen her and showed him her list of 'parties' in the building. 'There isn't any name on here except Mr Newton's,' she said smugly, 'that's why I sent you to the Cedar Suite.'

'Perhaps my father isn't dead at all,' said Patrick, leaning towards her; 'that really would be a shock. Maybe it was just a cry for help, what do you think?'

'I'd better go check with our director,' she said, retreating. 'Excuse me just one moment.' She opened a door concealed in one of the panels and slipped behind it.

Patrick leant against the counter, breathless with rage, among the black and white marble diamonds of the lobby floor. Just like the floor of that hall in Eaton Square. He had only been as high as the old lady's hand. She had clutched her cane, her prominent blue veins flowing down her fingers into a sapphire ring. Blood arrested and clarified. The old lady talked to his mother about their committee, while Patrick got lost in the feeling that he was making the resemblance happen. Now there were days when everything resembled everything else, and the smallest excuse for comparison made one object consume another in a bulimic feast.

What the fuck was going on? Why were his father's *remains* so hard to find? He had no trouble in discovering them in himself, it was only Frank E. MacDonald that was experiencing this difficulty. While Patrick cackled hysterically at this thought, a bald homosexual with a moustache, and a strong sense of the restrained flare he brought with him into the mortuary business, emerged from the panelled door and clicked his way across the black and white diamonds of the lobby floor. Without apology, he told Patrick to step right this way and led him back into the elevator. He pressed the button for the second floor, less near to heaven than Mr Newton, but without the sound of a cocktail party. In the silence of that discreetly lit corridor, the director mincing ahead of him, Patrick began to realise that he had wasted his defences on an impostor and, exhausted by the farce

23

of Mr Newton's wake, he was now dangerously vulnerable to the impact of his father's corpse.

'This is the room,' said the director, playing with his cuff. 'I'll leave you to be alone with him,' he purred.

Patrick glanced into the small, richly carpeted room. *Fucking hell*. What was his father doing in a coffin? He nodded to the director and waited outside the room, feeling a wave of madness rise up inside him. What did it mean that he was about to see his father's corpse? What was it meant to mean? He hovered in the doorway. His father's head was lying towards him and he could not yet see the face, just the grey curls of his hair. They had covered the body with tissue paper. It lay in the coffin, like a present someone had put down half-way through unwrapping.

'It's Dad!' muttered Patrick incredulously, clasping his hands together and turning to an imaginary friend. 'You *shouldn't* have!'

He stepped into the room, filled with dread again, but driven by curiosity. The face, alas, had not been covered in tissue, and Patrick was amazed by the nobility of his father's countenance. Those looks, which had deceived so many people because they were disconnected from his father's personality, were all the more impertinent now that the disconnection was complete. His father looked as if death was an enthusiasm he did not share, but with which he had been surrounded like a priest at a boxing match.

Those bruised, flickering eyes that assessed every weakness, like a teller's fingers counting a stack of banknotes, were now closed. That underlip, so often thrust out before a burst of anger, now contradicted the proud expression into which his features had relaxed. It had been torn open (he must have still been wearing his false teeth) by rage and protest and the consciousness of death.

However closely he tracked his father's life – and he felt the influence of this habit like a pollution in his bloodstream, a poison he had not put there himself, impossible to purge or leech without draining the patient – however closely he tried to imagine the lethal combination of pride and cruelty and sadness which had dominated his father's life, and however much he longed for it not to dominate his own life, Patrick could never follow him into that final moment when he had known he was about to die and he had been right. (Patrick had known he was about to die often enough, but he had always been wrong.)

Patrick felt a strong desire to take his father's lip in both hands and tear it like a piece of paper, along the gash already made by his teeth.

No, not that. He would not have that thought. The obscene necessity of going over the curtain-pole. Not that, he would not have that thought. Nobody should do that to anybody else. He could not be that person. Bastard.

Patrick growled, his teeth bared and clenched. He

punched the side of the coffin with his knuckles to bring him round. How should he play this scene from the movie of his life? He straightened himself and smiled contemptuously.

'Dad,' he said in his most cloying American accent, 'you were so fucking sad, man, and now you're trying to make me sad too.' He choked insincerely. 'Well,' he added in his own voice, 'bad luck.'

CHAPTER THREE

Anne Eisen turned into her building, carrying a box of cakes from Le Vrai Pâtisserie. If it had been La Vraie Pâtisserie, as Victor never tired of pointing out, it would have been even vraie-er, or *plus* vraie, she thought, smiling at Fred the doorman. Fred looked like a boy who had inherited his older brother's school uniform. The gold-braided sleeves of his brown coat hung down to the knuckles of his big pale hands, whereas his trousers, defeated by the bulk of his buttocks and thighs, flapped high above the pale blue nylon socks that clung to his ankles.

'Hi, Fred,' said Anne.

'Hello, Mrs Eisen, can I help you with your packages?' said Fred, waddling over.

'Thanks,' said Anne, stooping theatrically, 'but I can still manage two millefeuilles and a *pain au raisin*. Say, Fred,' she added, 'I have a friend coming over round four o'clock. He's young and sort of ill-looking. Be gentle with him, his father just died.'

'Oh, gee, I'm sorry,' said Fred.

'I don't think *he* is,' said Anne, 'although he may not know that yet.'

Fred tried to look as if he hadn't heard. Mrs Eisen was a real nice lady, but sometimes she said the weirdest things.

Anne got into the lift and pressed the button for the eleventh floor. In a few weeks it would all be over. No more eleventh floor, no more of Professor Wilson's cane chairs and his African masks and his big abstract I-think-it's-good-but-his-work-never-really-caught-on painting in the drawing room.

Jim Wilson, whose rich wife enabled him to exhibit his rather old-fashioned liberal wares on Park Avenue, no less, had been 'visiting' Oxford since October, while Victor visited Columbia in exchange. Every time Anne and Victor went to a party – and they almost never stopped – she'd needle him about being the visiting Professor. Anne and Victor had an 'open' marriage. 'Open', as in 'open wound' or 'open rebellion' or indeed 'open marriage', was not always a good thing, but now that Victor was seventy-six it hardly seemed worth divorcing him. Besides, somebody had to look after him.

Anne got out of the lift and opened the door to Apartment 11E, reaching for the light switch, next to the Red Indian blanket that hung in the hall. What the hell was she going to say to Patrick? Although he had turned into a surly and malicious adolescent, and was now a drug-addled twenty-two-year-old, she could still remember him sitting on the stairs at

Lacoste when he was five, and she still felt responsible – she knew it was absurd – for not managing to get his mother away from that gruesome dinner party.

Oddly enough, the delusions which had enabled her to marry Victor had really started on that evening. During the next few months Victor immersed himself in the creation of his new book, *Being, Knowing and Judging*, so easily (and yet so wrongly!) confused with its predecessor *Thinking, Knowing and Judging*. Victor's claim that he wanted to keep his students 'on their toes' by giving his books such similar titles, had not altogether extinguished Anne's doubts or those of his publisher. Nevertheless, like a masterful broom, his new book had scattered the dust long settled on the subject of identity, and swept it into exciting new piles.

At the end of this creative surge Victor had proposed to Anne. She had been thirty-four and, although she didn't know it at the time, her admiration for Victor was at its peak. She had accepted him, not only because he was imbued with that mild celebrity which is all a living philosopher can hope for, but also because she believed that Victor was a good man.

What the hell was she going to say to Patrick? she wondered as she took a spinach-green majolica plate from Barbara's fabulous collection and arranged the cakes on its irregularly glazed surface.

It was no use pretending to Patrick that she had liked David Melrose. Even after his divorce from

29

Eleanor, when he was poor and ill, David had been no more endearing than a chained alsatian. His life was an unblemished failure and his isolation terrifying to imagine, but he still had a smile like a knife; and if he had tried to learn (talk about a mature student!) how to please people, his efforts were faintly repulsive to anyone who knew his real nature.

As she leant over an annoyingly low Moroccan table in the drawing room, Anne felt her dark glasses slip from the top of her head. Perhaps her yellow cotton dress was a little too upbeat for the occasion, but what the hell? Patrick had not seen her recently enough to tell that she had dyed her hair. No doubt Barbara Wilson would have let it go naturally grey, but Anne had to appear on television tomorrow night to talk about 'The New Woman'. While she had been trying to find out what on earth a New Woman might be, she had got a New hairstyle and bought a New dress. It was research and she wanted expenses.

Twenty to four. Dead time until he arrived. Time to light a lethal, cancer-causing cigarette, time to fly in the face of the Surgeon General's advice – as if you could trust a man who was a surgeon and a general at the same time. She called that working both sides of the street. There was no disguising it, though, she *did* feel guilty, but then she felt guilty putting three drops of bath essence into the water instead of two. So what the hell?

Anne had barely lit her mild, light, mentholated,

30

almost entirely pointless cigarette, when the buzzer rang from downstairs.

'Hi, Fred.'

'Oh, hello, Mrs Eisen. Mr Melrose is here.'

'Well, I guess you'd better send him up,' she said, wondering if there wasn't some way they could ever vary this conversation.

Anne went into the kitchen, switched on the kettle, and sprinkled some tea-leaves into the Japanese teapot with the wobbly overarching rattan handle.

The doorbell interrupted her and she hurried out of the kitchen to open the front door. Patrick was standing with his back to her in a long black overcoat.

'Hello, Patrick,' she said.

'Hello,' he mumbled, trying to squeeze past her. But she took him by the shoulders and embraced him warmly.

'I'm so sorry,' she said.

Patrick would not yield to this embrace, but slid away like a wrestler breaking an opponent's grip.

'I'm sorry too,' he said, bowing slightly. 'Being late is a bore, but arriving early is unforgivable. Punctuality is one of the smaller vices I've inherited from my father; it means I'll never really be chic.' He paced up and down the drawing room with his hands in his overcoat pockets. '*Unlike* this apartment,' he sneered. 'Who was lucky enough to swap this place for your nice house in London?'

'Victor's opposite number at Columbia, Jim Wilson.'

31

'God, imagine having an opposite number instead of always being one's own opposite number,' said Patrick.

'Do you want some tea?' asked Anne with a sympathetic sigh.

'Hum,' said Patrick. 'I wonder if I could have a real drink as well? For me it's already nine in the evening.'

'For you it's always nine in the evening,' said Anne. 'What do you want? I'll fix it for you.'

'No, I'll do it,' he said, 'you won't make it strong enough.'

'Okay,' said Anne, turning towards the kitchen, 'the drinks are on the Mexican millstone.'

The millstone was engraved with feathered warriors, but it was the bottle of Wild Turkey which commanded Patrick's attention. He poured some into a tall glass and knocked back another Quaalude with the first gulp, refilling the glass immediately. After seeing his father's corpse, he had gone to the Forty-fourth Street branch of the Morgan Guaranty Bank and collected three thousand dollars in cash which now bulged inside an orange-brown envelope in his pocket.

He checked the pills again (lower right pocket) and then the envelope (inside left) and then the credit cards (outer left). This nervous action, which he sometimes performed every few minutes, was like a man crossing himself before an altar – The Drugs: The Cash: and The Holy Ghost of Credit.

He had already taken a second Quaalude after the visit to the bank, but he still felt groundless and desperate and overwrought. Perhaps a third one was overdoing it, but overdoing it was his occupation.

'Does this happen to you?' asked Patrick, striding into the kitchen with renewed energy. 'You see a millstone, and the words "round my neck" ring up like the price on an old cash register. Isn't it humiliating,' he said, taking some ice cubes, ' – God, I love these ice machines, they're the best thing about America so far – humiliating that one's thoughts have all been prepared in advance by these idiotic mechanisms?'

'The idiotic ones aren't good,' Anne agreed, 'but there's no need for the cash register to come up with something cheap.'

'If your mind works like a cash register, anything you come up with is bound to be cheap.'

'You obviously don't shop at Le Vrai Pâtisserie,' said Ann, carrying the cakes and tea into the drawing room.

'If we can't control our conscious responses, what chance do we have against the influences we haven't recognised?'

'None at all,' said Anne cheerfully, handing him a cup of tea.

Patrick let loose a curt laugh. He felt detached from what he had been saying. Perhaps the Quaaludes were beginning to make a difference.

'Do you want a cake?' said Anne. 'I bought them

to remind us of Lacoste. They're as French as . . . as French letters.'

'That French,' gasped Patrick, taking one of the millefeuilles out of politeness. As he picked it up, the cake oozed cream from its flanks, like pus dribbling from a wound. Christ, he thought, this cake is completely *out of control*.

'It's *alive*!' he said out loud, squeezing the millefeuille rather too hard. Cream spurted out and dropped on to the elaborate brass surface of the Moroccan table. His fingers were sticky with icing. 'Oh, I'm sorry,' he mumbled, putting the cake down.

Anne handed him a napkin. She noticed that Patrick was becoming increasingly clumsy and slurred. Before he had arrived she was dreading the inevitable conversation about his father; now she was worried that it might not take place.

'Have you been to see your father yet?' she asked outright.

'I did see him,' said Patrick without hesitation. 'I thought he was at his best in a coffin – so much less difficult than usual.' He grinned at her disarmingly.

Anne smiled at him faintly, but Patrick needed no encouragement.

'When I was young,' he said, 'my father used to take us to restaurants. I say "restaurants" in the plural, because we never stormed in and out of less than three. Either the menu took too long to arrive, or a waiter struck my father as intolerably stupid, or the wine list disappointed him. I remember he once held a bottle of red wine upside down while the contents gurgled out on to the carpet. "How dare you bring me this filth?" he shouted. The waiter was so frightened that instead of throwing him out, he brought more wine.'

'So you liked being with him in a place he didn't complain about.'

'Exactly,' said Patrick. 'I couldn't believe my luck, and for a while I expected him to sit up in his coffin, like a vampire at sunset, and say, "The service here is intolerable." Then we would have had to go to three or four other funeral parlours. Mind you, the service *was* intolerable. They sent me to the wrong corpse.'

'The wrong corpse!' exclaimed Anne.

'Yes, I wound up at a jaunty Jewish cocktail party given for a Mr Hermann Newton. I wish I could have stayed; they seemed to be having such fun.'

'What an appalling story,' said Anne, lighting a cigarette. 'I'll bet they give courses in Bereavement Counselling.'

'Of course,' said Patrick, letting out another quick hollow laugh and sinking back into his armchair. He could definitely feel the influence of the Quaaludes now. The alcohol had brought out the best in them, like the sun coaxing open the petals of a flower, he reflected tenderly.

'I'm sorry?' he said. He had not heard Anne's last question.

'Is he being cremated?' she repeated.

'Yes, that's right,' said Patrick. 'I gather that when people are cremated one never really gets their ashes, just some communal rakings from the bottom of the oven. As you can imagine, I regard that as good news. Ideally, *all* the ashes would belong to somebody else, but we don't live in a perfect world.'

Anne had given up wondering whether he was sorry about his father's death, and had started wishing he was a little sorrier. His venemous remarks, although they could not affect David, made Patrick look so ill he might have been waiting to die from a snake bite.

Patrick closed his eyes slowly and, after a very long time, slowly opened them again. The whole operation took about half an hour. Another half an hour elapsed while he licked his dry and fascinatingly sore lips. He was really getting something off that last Quaalude. His blood was hissing like a television screen after closedown. His hands were like dumb-bells, like dumb-bells in his hands. Everything folding inwards and growing heavier.

'Hello there!' Anne called.

'I'm so sorry,' said Patrick, leaning forward with what he imagined was a charming smile. 'I'm awfully tired.'

'Maybe you ought to go to bed.'

'No, no, no. Let's not exaggerate.'

'You could lie down for a few hours,' Anne suggested, 'and then have dinner with Victor and me. We're going to a party afterwards, given by some ghastly Long Island Anglophiles. Just your kind of thing.'

'It's sweet of you, but I really can't face too many strangers at the moment,' said Patrick, playing his bereavement card a little too late to convince Anne.

'You should come along,' she coaxed. 'I'm sure it will be an example of "unashamed luxury".'

'I can't imagine what that means,' said Patrick sleepily.

'Let me give you the address anyhow,' Anne insisted. 'I don't like the idea of your being alone too much.'

'Fine. Write it down for me before I go.'

He knew he had to take some speed soon or involuntarily take up Anne's offer to 'lie down for a few hours'. He did not want to swallow a whole Beauty, because it would take him on a fifteen-hour megalomaniac odyssey, and he didn't want to be *that* conscious. On the other hand, he had to get rid of the feeling that he had been dropped into a pool of slowly drying concrete.

'Where's the loo?'

Anne told him how to get there, and Patrick waded across the carpet in the direction she had indicated.

Once he had locked the bathroom door Patrick felt a familiar sense of security. Inside a bathroom he could give in to the obsession with his own physical and mental state which was so often compromised by the presence of other people or the absence of a well-lit mirror. Most of the 'quality time' in his life had been spent in a bathroom. Injecting, snorting, swallowing, stealing, overdosing; examining his pupils, his arms, his tongue, his stash.

'Oh, bathrooms!' he intoned, spreading out his arms in front of the mirror. 'Thy medicine cabinets pleaseth me mightily! Thy towels moppeth up the rivers of my blood . . .' He petered out as he took the Black Beauty from his pocket. He was just going to take enough to function, just enough to . . . what had he been about to say? He couldn't remember. My God, it was short-term memory loss again, the Professor Moriarty of drug abuse, interrupting and then obliterating the precious sensations one went to such trouble to secure.

'Inhuman fiend,' he muttered.

The black capsule eventually came apart and he emptied half the contents onto one of the Portuguese tiles around the basin. Taking out one of his new hundred-dollar notes, he rolled it into a tight tube and sniffed up the small heap of white powder from the tile.

His nose stung and his eyes watered slightly but, refusing to be distracted, Patrick resealed the capsule, wrapped it in a Kleenex, put it back in his pocket and then, for no reason he could identify, almost against his will, he took it out again, emptied the rest of the powder onto a tile and sniffed it up as well. The effects wouldn't last so long this way, he argued, inhaling deeply through his nose. It was too sordid to take half of anything. Anyhow, his father had just died and he was entitled to be confused. The main thing, the heroic feat, the proof of his seriousness and his samurai status in the war against drugs, was that he hadn't taken any heroin.

Patrick leant forward and checked his pupils in the mirror. They had definitely dilated. His heartbeat had accelerated. He felt invigorated, he felt refreshed, in fact he felt rather aggressive. It was as if he had never taken a drink or a drug, he was back in complete control, the lighthouse beams of speed cutting through the thick night of the Quaaludes and the alcohol and the jet lag.

'And,' he said, clasping his lapels with mayorial solemnity, 'last but not least, through the dark shadow, if I might put it thus, of our grief for the passing away of David Melrose.'

How long had he been in the bathroom? It seemed like a lifetime. The fire brigade would probably be forcing the door down soon. Patrick started to clear up hastily. He didn't want to put the shell of the Black Beauty into the waste-paper basket (paranoia!) and so he forced the two halves of the empty capsule down the basin plug-hole. How was he going to explain his reanimated state to Anne? He splashed some cold water on his face and left it ostentatiously dripping. There was only one thing left to do: that authentic-sounding flush with which every junkie leaves a bathroom, hoping to deceive the audience that crowds his imagination.

'For God's sake,' said Anne when he got back to the drawing room, 'why don't you dry your face?'

'I was just reviving myself with a little cold water.'

'Oh yeah?' said Anne. 'What kind of water was that?'

'Very refreshing water,' he said, wiping his sweaty palms on his trousers as he sat down. 'Which reminds me,' he said, getting up immediately, 'I'd love another drink if I may.'

'Sure,' said Anne resignedly. 'By the way, I forgot to ask, how is Debbie?'

The question filled Patrick with the horror which assailed him when he was asked to consider another person's feelings. How was Debbie? How the fuck should he know? It was hard enough to rescue himself from the avalanche of his own feelings, without allowing the gloomy St Bernard of his attention to wander into other fields. On the other hand the amphetamines had given him an urgent desire to talk and he couldn't ignore the question entirely.

'Well,' he said from the other side of the room, 'she's following in her mothers footsteps, and writing an article about great hostesses. Teresa Hickmann's footsteps, invisible to most people, glow in the dark for her dutiful daughter. Still, we should be grateful that she hasn't modelled her conversational style on her father's.'

Patrick was momentarily lost again in the contemplation of his psychological state. He felt lucid, but not about anything, except his own lucidity. His thoughts, anticipating themselves hopelessly, stuttered in the starting blocks, and brought his feeling of fluency dangerously close to silence. 'But you haven't told me,' he said, tearing himself away from this intriguing mental stammer and at the same time taking his revenge on Anne for asking him about Debbie, 'how is Victor?'

'Oh, fine. He's a grand old man now, a role he's been training for all his life. He gets a lot of attention and he's lecturing on Identity, which, as he says, he can do with his eyes closed. Did you ever read *Being, Knowing and Judging*'

'No,' said Patrick.

'Well, I must give you a copy then,' said Anne, getting up and going to the bookshelves. She took out what looked to Patrick like a tiresomely thick volume from among half a dozen copies of the same book. He liked slim books which he could slip into his overcoat pocket and leave there unread for months. What was the point of a book if you couldn't carry it around with you as a theoretical defence against boredom?

'It's about identity, is it?' he asked suspiciously.

'All you've ever wanted to know but never dared to formulate precisely,' said Anne.

'Goody,' said Patrick, getting up restlessly. He had to pace, he had to move through space, otherwise the world had a dangerous tendency to flatten itself and he felt like a fly crawling up a window-pane looking for a way out of its translucent prison. Anne,

41

thinking he had come to fetch it, handed him the book.

'Oh, eh, thank you,' he said, leaning over to kiss her quickly, 'I'll read it very soon.'

He tried to stuff the book into his overcoat pocket. He had *known* it wasn't going to fit. It was completely fucking useless. Now he had to carry this stupid fat book round with him everywhere. He felt a wave of violent rage. He stared intensely at a waste-paper basket (once a Somalian water jug) and imagined the book spinning towards it like a frisbee.

'I really ought to be going now,' he said curtly.

'Really? Won't you stay to say hello to Victor?'

'No, I must go,' he said impatiently.

'Okay, but let me give you Samantha's address.'

'What?'

'The party.'

'Oh, yes. I doubt I'll come,' said Patrick.

Anne wrote down the address on a piece of paper and handed it to Patrick. 'There you are.'

'Thank you,' said Patrick abruptly, flicking up the collar of his overcoat. 'I'll call you tomorrow.'

'Or see you tonight.'

'Maybe.'

He turned around and hurried towards the door. He had to get outside. His heart seemed to be about to leap out of his chest, like a jack-in-the-box, and he felt that he could only force the lid down for a few seconds more.

'Goodbye,' he called from the door.

42

'Goodbye,' said Anne.

Down in the sluggish airless lift, past the fat moronic doorman, and into the street. The shock of standing again under that wide pale sky, completely *exposed*. This must be what the oyster feels when the lemon juice falls.

Why had he left the shelter of Anne's flat? And so rudely. Now she would hate him for ever. Everything he did was wrong.

Patrick looked down the avenue. It was like the opening shot of a documentary on overpopulation. He walked down the street, imagining the severed heads of passers-by rolling into the gutter in his wake.

CHAPTER FOUR

How could he think his way out of the problem when the problem was the way he
thought? Patrick wondered, not for the first
time, as he slipped reluctantly out of his overcoat and
handed it to a brilliantined red-jacketed waiter.

Eating was only a temporary solution. But then all
solutions were temporary, even death, and nothing
gave him more faith in the existence of an afterlife
than the inexorable sarcasm of Fate. No doubt suicide
would turn out to be the violent preface to yet
another span of nauseating consciousness, of dimin-
ishing spirals and tightening nooses, and memories
like shrapnel tearing all day long through his flesh.
Who could guess what exquisite torments lay ahead
in the holiday camps of eternity? It almost made one
grateful to be alive.

Only behind a waterfall of brutal and pleasurable
sensations, thought Patrick, accepting the leather-
clad menu without bothering to glance up, could he
hide from the bloodhounds of his conscience. There,
in the cool recess of the rock, behind that heavy

white veil, he would hear them yelping and snarling confusedly on the river bank, but at least they couldn't tear out his throat with the fury of their reproach. After all, the trail he'd left was not hard to follow. It was littered with the evidence of wasted time and hopeless longing, not to mention those blood-stained shirts, and the syringes whose spikes he had bent in a fit of disgust and then unbent again for one last fix. Patrick drew in his breath sharply and folded his arms over his chest.

'A dry Martini. Straight up, with a twist,' he drawled. 'And I'm ready to order.'

A waiter was coming right on over to take his order. Everything was under control.

Most people who were withdrawing and speeding, jet-lagged and cudgelled by Quaaludes, might have lost their interest in food, but Patrick found that all his appetites were operational at all times, even when his loathing of being touched gave his desire for sex a theoretical complexion.

He could remember Johnny Hall saying indignantly of a girlfriend he had recently thrown out, 'She was just the kind of girl who came over and ruffled your hair when you'd just had a fix of coke.' Patrick had howled at the horror of such a tactless act. When a man is feeling as empty and fragile as a pane of glass, he does not want to have his hair ruffled. There could be no negotiation between people who thought that cocaine was a vaguely naughty and salacious drug, and the intravenous addict who knew that it was an opportunity to experience the arctic landscape of pure terror.

That terror was the price he had to pay for the first heartbreaking wave of pleasure when consciousness seemed to burst out, like white blossoms, along the branches of every nerve. And all his scattered thoughts came rushing together, like loose iron filings as a magnet is held over them and draws them into the shape of a rose. Or – he must stop thinking about it – or like a solution of saturated copper sulphate under the microscope, when it suddenly transforms and crystals break out everywhere on its surface.

He must stop thinking about it – and do it. No! And think about something else. His father's corpse, for instance. Would that be an improvement? It would get rid of the problem of desire, but hatred could be compulsive too.

Ah, here was the Dry Martini. If not the cavalry, at least some more ammunition. Patrick drained the cold unctuous liquid in one gulp.

'Would you care for another one, sir?'

'Yes,' said Patrick brusquely.

A more senior waiter in a dinner-jacket came over to take Patrick's order.

'Tartare de Saumon Cru, followed by the Steak Tartare,' said Patrick, taking an innocent pleasure in saying 'Tartare' twice and pleased to be ordering two adult forms of baby food, already cut up and squished together for him.

A third waiter, with a golden bunch of grapes in his lapel, and a large golden wine-tasting cup dangling from a chain around his neck, was only too ready to bring Patrick a bottle of Corton Charlemagne straight away and to open a bottle of Ducru-Beaucaillou for later on. Everything was under control.

No, he mustn't think about it, or indeed about anything, and especially not about heroin, because heroin was the only thing that really worked, the only thing that stopped him scampering around in a hamster's wheel of unanswerable questions. Heroin was the cavalry. Heroin was the missing chair leg, made with such precision that it matched every splinter of the break. Heroin landed purring at the base of his skull, and wrapped itself darkly around his nervous system, like a black cat curling up on its favourite cushion. It was as soft and rich as the throat of a wood pigeon, or the splash of sealing wax onto a page, or a handful of gems slipping from palm to palm.

The way other people felt about love, he felt about heroin, and he felt about love the way other people felt about heroin: that it was a dangerous and incomprehensible waste of time. What could he say to Debbie? 'Although you know that my hatred for my father, and my love for drugs, are the most important relationships in my life, I want you to know that you come in third.' What woman would not be proud to be 'among the medals' in such a contest?

'Oh, for fuck's sake shut up,' mumbled Patrick out loud, drinking his second dry martini with as little restraint as the first. If things went on this way he would have to call Pierre, his truly wonderful New York dealer. No! He wasn't going to do it, he had sworn that he wasn't going to do it. 243–1726. The number might as well have been tattooed on his wrist. He hadn't rung it since September, eight months ago, but he would never forget the bowel-loosening excitement of those seven digits.

Golden Grapes was back, peeling the heavy yellow lead from the neck of the Corton Charlemagne, and cradling the bottle of claret, while Patrick studied the picture of a white château under a flat gold sky. Perhaps with these consolations he would not have to score after dinner, thought Patrick sceptically, sucking a sample of Corton Charlemagne into his mouth.

The first taste made him break into a grin of recognition, like a man who has sighted his lover at the end of a crowded platform. Raising the glass again, he took a large gulp of the pale yellow wine, held it in his mouth for a few seconds and then let it slide down his throat. Yes, it worked, it still worked. Some things never let him down.

He closed his eyes and the taste rippled over him like an hallucination. Cheaper wine would have buried him in fruit, but the grapes he imagined now were mercifully artificial, like earrings of swollen yellow pearls. He pictured the long sinewy shoots of the vine, dragging him down into the heavy reddish soil. Traces of iron and stone and earth and rain flashed across his palate and tantalised him like shooting stars. Sensations long wrapped in a bottle now unfurled like a stolen canvas.

Some things never let him down. It made him want to cry.

'Would you care to taste the Do-crew Bo-ca-u?'

'Yes,' said Patrick.

Golden Grapes poured the red wine into a ludicrously large glass. Even the smell of it made Patrick see things. Glistening granite. Cobwebs. Gothic cellars.

'That's fine,' he said, without bothering to taste it. 'Pour some now, I'll drink it later.'

Patrick sank back in his chair. Now that the wine distraction was over, the same question returned: would he go to his dealer after dinner, or to his hotel? Perhaps he could go to see Pierre socially. Patrick yelped with laughter at the absurdity of this pretext, but at the same time he felt a tremendous sentimental desire to see the demented Frenchman again. In many ways Pierre was the person Patrick felt closest to.

Pierre had spent eight years in a lunatic asylum under the misapprehension that he was an egg. 'For eight fucking years, man,' he would say, speaking very rapidly in a strong French accent, 'I thought I was an egg. *Je croyais que j'étais un oeuf* – it's no fucking joke.' During this time his deserted body was fed, moved, washed and clothed by nurses who had no idea that they were ministering to an egg. Pierre was let free to shoot about the world on unfettered voyages, in a state of enlightenment which did not require the crass mediation of words and senses. 'I understood everything,' he would say, glaring at Patrick defiantly. *J'avais une conscience totale.*

On these voyages, Pierre would occasionally stop by his hospital room and hover with pity and contempt over the as yet unhatched egg of his body. However, after eight years he realised that his body was dying of neglect.

'I had to force myself back into my fucking body; it was horrible. *J'avais un dégoût total.*'

Patrick was fascinated. It reminded him of Lucifer's disgust when he had to squeeze himself into the clammy and confining rings of the serpent's body.

One day the nurses came in with their sponges and their baby food, and found Pierre weak but impatient, sitting on the edge of his bed after almost a decade of inertia and silence.

'Okay, I go now,' he snapped.

Tests showed that he was perfectly lucid, perhaps too lucid, and so they discharged him from the hospital with relief.

Only a perpetual flow of heroin and cocaine could now sustain a coarse version of his former glorious insanity. He hovered, but not as lightly as before, on the margins between his body and his fatal nostalgia for disembodiment. In his arm a wound like a volcano cone, a scabrous mound of dried blood and scar

51

tissue, rose up from the soft hollow opposite his elbow. It enabled him to drop the thin spike of his insulin syringes vertically into the vein, never digging for a hit, but leaving open this access to his bloodstream, like an emergency runway, always ready for another speedball to relieve the horror of his incarceration in a jaundiced and inhospitable body he could hardly call his own.

Pierre's routine was perfectly regular. He stayed awake for two and a half days and then, after a big shot of heroin, slept or at least rested for eighteen hours. During his waking periods he sold drugs curtly and efficiently, allowing most of his customers no more than ten minutes in his black and white apartment. He also saved himself the inconvenience of people dying in his bathroom by banning injections, a prohibition he soon lifted for Patrick. Throughout the last summer Patrick had tried to keep to the same sleep patterns as Pierre. They often stayed up all night, sitting either side of the horizontal mirror Pierre used as a table, stripped to the waist to save themselves the trouble of rolling their sleeves up and down, shooting up every quarter of an hour and, as they poured with chemical-smelling sweat, talking about their favourite subjects: how to achieve perfect disembodiment; how to witness their own deaths; how to stay in the borderlands, undefined by the identities which their histories tried to thrust upon them; how dishonest and shallow all the straight people were; and, of course, how they could give up drugs if they really wanted to, a condition that had not so far afflicted either of them for very long.

Fucking hell, thought Patrick, draining his third glass of white wine and immediately reloading it from the dripping bottle. He *must* stop thinking about it.

With a father like his (sob, sob), Authority Figures and Role Models had always been a problem, but in Pierre he had at last found someone whose example he could follow with unqualified enthusiasm, and whose advice he could bear to take. At least until Pierre had tried to limit him to two grams of coke a day instead of the seven Patrick regarded as indispensable.

'You're fucking crazy, man,' Pierre had shouted at him, 'you go for the rush every time. You kill yourself that way.'

This argument had marred the end of the summer, but in any case it had been time to get rid of the inflamed rashes that covered Patrick's entire body and the burning white ulcers that had suddenly sprouted throughout his mouth, throat and stomach, and so he had returned to England a few days later to check into his favourite clinic.

'*Oh, les beaux jours,*' he sighed, wolfing down his raw salmon in a few breathless mouthfuls. He drank the last of the white wine, indifferent now to its taste.

Who else was in this ghastly restaurant? Extraordinary that he hadn't looked before; or not so extraordinary, in fact. They wouldn't be calling him in to

53

solve the Problem of Other Minds, although of course the people, like Victor, who thought it was a problem in the first place were famous for being entirely absorbed in the workings of their own minds. Strange coincidence.

He swivelled his eyes around the room with reptilian coldness. He hated them all, every single one, especially that incredibly fat man sitting with the blonde. He must have paid her to mask her disgust at being in his company.

'God, you're repulsive,' muttered Patrick. 'Have you ever considered going on a diet? Yes, that's right, a diet, or hasn't it crossed your mind that you're quite appallingly fat?' Patrick felt vindictively and loutishly aggressive. Alcohol is such a crude high, he thought, remembering the sage pronouncement of his first hash dealer from his schooldays, a zonked-out old hippy bore called Barry.

'If I looked like you,' he sneered at the fat man, 'I'd commit suicide. Not that one needs an incentive.'

There was no doubt about it, he was a fattist and sexist and an ageist and a racist and a straightist and a druggist and, naturally, a snob, but of such a virulent character that nobody satisfied his demands. He defied anyone to come up with a minority or a majority that he did not hate for some reason or another.

'Is everything okay, sir?' asked one of the waiters, mistaking Patrick's mutterings for an attempt to order.

54

'Yes, yes,' said Patrick. Well, not absolutely every-thing, he thought, you can't seriously expect anyone to agree to that. In fact the idea of everything being okay made him feel dangerously indignant. Affir-mation was too rare a commodity to waste on such a ludicrous statement. He felt like calling the waiter back to correct any false impression of happiness he might have created. But here was another waiter – would they never leave him alone? Could he bear it if they did? – bringing his Steak Tartare. He wanted it spicy, very spicy.

A couple of minutes later, his mouth seared with Tabasco and cayenne pepper, Patrick had already devoured the mound of raw meat and *pommes allumet-tes* on his plate.

'That's right, dear,' he said in his Nanny Voice, 'you get something solid inside you.'

'Yes, Nanny,' he replied obediently. 'Like a bullet, or a needle, eh, Nanny?'

'A bullet, indeed,' he huffed and puffed, 'a needle! Whatever next? You always were a strange boy. No good'll come of it, you mark my words, young man.'

Oh, God, it was starting. The endless voices. The solidarity dialogues. The dreadful jabbering that poured out uncontrollably. He gulped down an entire glass of red wine with an eagerness worthy of Law-rence of Arabia, as interpreted by Peter O'Toole, polishing off his glass of lemonade after a thirsty desert crossing. 'We've taken Aqaba,' he said, staring madly into space and twitching his eyebrows expertly.

'Would you care for a dessert, sir?'

At last, a real person with a real question, albeit a rather bizarre question. How was he supposed to 'care for' a dessert? Did he have to visit it on Sundays? Send it a Christmas card? Did he have to feed it?

'Yeah,' said Patrick, smiling wildly, 'I'll have a Crème Brûlée.'

Patrick stared at his glass. The red wine was definitely beginning to unfold. Pity he had already drunk it all. Yes, it had been beginning to unfold, like a fist opening slowly. And in its palm . . . In its palm, what? A ruby? A grape? A stone? Perhaps similes just shunted the same idea back and forth, lightly disguised, to give the impression of a fruitful trade.

Sir Sampson Legend was the only honest suitor who ever sang the praises of a woman. 'Give me your hand, Odd, let me kiss it; 'tis as warm and as soft – as what? – Odd, as t'other hand.' Now there was an accurate simile. The tragic limitations of comparison. The lead in the heart of the skylark. The disappointing curvature of space. The doom of time.

Christ, he was really quite drunk. Not drunk enough, though. He poured the stuff in, but it didn't reach the root-confusions, the accident by the roadside, still trapped in the buckling metal after all these years. He sighed loudly, ending in a kind of grunt, and bowing his head hopelessly.

The Crème Brûlée arrived and he gobbled it down

with the same desperate impatience he showed towards all food, but now edged with weariness and oppression. His violent way of eating always left him in a state of speechless sadness at the end of a meal. After several minutes during which he could only stare at the foot of his glass, he summoned enough passion to order some Marc de Bourgogne and the bill.

Patrick closed his eyes and let the cigarette smoke drift out of his mouth and up into his nose and out through his mouth again. This was recycling at its best. Of course he could still go to the party Anne had invited him to, but he knew that he wouldn't. Why did he always refuse? Refuse to participate. Refuse to agree. Refuse to forgive. Once it was too late he would long to have gone to this party. He glanced at his watch. Only nine-thirty. The time had not yet come, but the moment it did, refusal would turn into regret. He could even imagine loving a woman if he had lost her first.

With reading it was the same thing. As soon as he was deprived of books, his longing to read became insatiable, whereas if he took the precaution of carrying a book with him, as he had this evening, slipping *The Myth of Sysyphus* yet again into his overcoat pocket, then he could be sure that he would not be troubled by a desire for literature.

Before *The Myth of Sysyphus* he had carried round *The Unnamable* and *Nightwood* for at least a year, and for two years before that the ultimate overcoat book,

The Heart of Darkness. Sometimes, driven on by horror at his own ignorance and a determination to conquer a difficult book, or even a seminal text, he would take a copy of something like *Seven Types of Ambiguity* or *The Decline and Fall of the Roman Empire* out of his bookshelves only to find that its opening pages were already covered in spidery and obscure annotations in his own handwriting. These traces of an earlier civilisation would have reassured him if he had any recollection at all of the things he had obviously once read, but this forgetfulness made him panic instead. What was the point of an experience if it eluded him so thoroughly? His past seemed to turn to water in his cupped hands and to slip irretrievably through his nervous fingers.

Patrick heaved himself up and walked across the thick red carpet of the restaurant, his head thrown back precariously and his eyes so nearly closed that the tables were dark blurs through the mesh of his eyelashes.

He had made a big decision. He would telephone Pierre and leave it to fate whether he scored or not. If Pierre was asleep then he would not get any smack, but if he was awake it was worth going round to get just enough for a good night's rest. And a little for the morning so he didn't feel sick.

The barman put a telephone down on the mahogany counter, and beside it a second Marc. 2 . . . 4 . . . 3 . . . 1 . . . 7 . . . 2 . . . 6. Patrick's heart rate increased; he suddenly felt alert.

'I cannot come to the phone right now, but if you leave . . .'

Patrick slammed the phone down. It was the fucking machine. What was he doing asleep at ten in the evening? It was absolutely intolerable. He picked the phone up and dialled the number again. Should he leave a message? Something subtly coded like 'Wake up, fuckface, I want to score.'

No, it was hopeless. Fate had spoken and he must accept its judgement.

Outside it was surprisingly warm. Nevertheless, Patrick flicked up the collar of his overcoat, scanning the street for a free cab.

He soon spotted a taxi and stepped into the street to hail it.

'The Pierre Hotel,' he said as he climbed inside.

CHAPTER FIVE

What instrument could he use to set himself free? Disdain? Aggression? Hatred? They were all contaminated by the influence of his father, the very thing he needed to free himself from. And the sadness he felt, if he paused for a second, had he not learnt it from his father's descent into paralysing misery?

After his divorce from Eleanor, David had remained in the South of France, only fifteen miles away from the old house in Lacoste. In his new house, which had no exterior windows, only windows looking onto a central weed-choked courtyard, he lay in bed for days on end wheezing and staring at the ceiling fixedly, without even the energy to cross the room and get the copy of *Jorrocks Rides Again* which had once been able to cheer him up in the most unpromising circumstances.

When Patrick, aged eight or nine, and torn between terror and unfathomable loyalty, visited his father, the enormous silences were only broken for

David to express a desire to die, and to issue his final instructions.

'I may not be alive for much longer,' he would gasp, 'and we may not see each other again.'

'No, Daddy, don't say that,' Patrick would plead with him.

And then the old exhortations would come out: observe everything . . . trust nobody . . . despise your mother . . . effort is vulgar . . . things were better in the eighteenth century.

Impressed by the thought, year after year, that these might be his father's last pronouncements on the world, the distillation of all his wisdom and experience, Patrick paid undue attention to this tiresome set of opinions, despite the overwhelming evidence that they had not got his father very far in the pursuit of happiness. But then that was vulgar too. The whole system worked beautifully, like so many others, after the initial leap of faith.

If his father ever managed to get out of bed, things got worse. They would walk down to the village on a shopping expedition, his father dressed in an old pair of green pyjamas, a short blue overcoat with anchors on the buttons, a pair of dark glasses now tied to a coarse string around his neck, and on his feet the heavy lace-up boots favoured by the local tractor-driving peasants. David had also grown a snow-white beard and always carried with him an orange nylon shopping bag with a tarnished gold handle. Patrick was mistaken for his grandson, and he could remember the shame and horror, as well as the defensive pride, with which he accompanied his increasingly eccentric and depressed father into the village.

'I want to die . . . I want to die . . . I want to die,' muttered Patrick rapidly. It was completely unacceptable. He could not be the person who had been that person. The speed was coming back and bringing with it the menace of lucidity and strong emotion.

They were approaching the hotel and Patrick had to make a quick decision. He leant forward and said to the driver, 'I've changed my mind, take me to Eighth Street between C and D.'

The Chinese driver looked doubtfully in his rear-view mirror. Avenue D was a far cry from the Pierre Hotel. What sort of man would suddenly veer from one to the other? Only a junkie or an ignorant tourist.

'Avenue D bad place,' he said, testing the second theory.

'I'm relying on that,' said Patrick. 'Just take me there.'

The driver carried on down Fifth Avenue, past the turning for the hotel. Patrick sank back, excited and sick and guilty, but masking the feeling, as usual, with a show of languid indifference.

So what if he had changed his mind? Flexibility was an admirable quality. And nobody was more flexible when it came to giving up drugs, nobody more open to the possibility of taking them after all.

He hadn't done anything yet. He could still reverse

his decision, or rather reverse his revision. He could still go back.

Plummeting from the Upper to the Lower East Side, from Le Veau Gras to the Bargain Grocery Store on Eighth Street, he could not help admiring the way he ranged freely, or perhaps the word was 'inevitably', between luxury and squalor.

The taxi was approaching Tompkins Square, the beginning of the fun district. It was here that Chilly Willy, his street contact for those annoying occasions on which Pierre was asleep, dragged out his life of perpetual withdrawal. Chilly could only ever get enough smack to keep him looking for more; scavenging enough bags to twitch instead of convulsing, to squeal instead of screaming, he walked in little jerky steps with one limp and nerveless arm dangling by his side, like an old flex from the draughty ceiling. With his good hand, Chilly held up the filthy baggy trousers that were always in danger of slipping down over his emaciated waist. Despite being black, he looked pale and his face was speckled with brown liver spots. His teeth, the four or five that still clung heroically to his gums, were either dark yellow or black, chipped or shattered. He was an inspiration to his community and his customers since nobody could imagine looking as ill as him, however recklessly they lived.

The cab crossed Avenue C and carried on down Eighth Street. Here he was among the filthy haunches of the city, thought Patrick contentedly.

'Where you want?' asked the Chinaman.

'I want heroin,' said Patrick.

'Heloin,' repeated the driver anxiously.

'That's right,' said Patrick. 'Stop here, this is good.'

Wired Puerto Ricans were pacing about pugilistically on the corner, and black guys with big hats were leaning in doorways. Patrick lowered the window of the taxi, and new friends crowded in from every side.

'What ju wan, man? What ju looking for?'

'Clear tape . . . red tape . . . yellow tape. What you want?'

'Smack,' said Patrick.

'Shit, man, you from the police. You're a policeman.'

'No, I'm not. I'm an Englishman,' Patrick protested.

'Get out the cab, man, we don't sell you notin' in the cab.'

'Wait here,' said Patrick to the driver. He got out of the taxi. One of the dealers took him by the arm and started to march him round the corner.

'I'm not going any further,' said Patrick as they were about to lose sight of the taxi.

'How much you want?'

'Give me four dime-bags of clear tape,' said Patrick, carefully unpeeling two twenty-dollar bills. He kept the twenties in the left trouser pocket, tens in the right trouser pocket, fives and ones in the overcoat pockets. The hundreds remained in their envelope in the inside coat pocket. This way he never tempted anybody with a show of cash.

'I'll give you six for fifty, man. You git one extra bag.'

'No, four is fine.'

Patrick pocketed the four little bags of grease-proof paper, turned around and climbed back into the cab.

'We go hotel now,' said the Chinaman eagerly.

'No, just drive me round the block for a bit. Take me to Sixth and B.'

'What you go lound block for?' The driver mumbled a Chinese curse, but moved off in the right direction.

Patrick had to test the smack he had just bought before he left the area altogether. He tore open one of the bags and poured the powder into the hollow formed in the back of his hand by the tendon of his raised thumb. He raised the tiny quantity of white powder to his nose and sniffed it up.

Oh, God! It was vile. Patrick clutched his stinging nose. Fuck, wank, blast, shit, damn.

It was a hideous cocktail of Vim and barbs. The scouring powder gave that touch of genuine bitterness to the mix, and the barbiturates provided a small thud of sedation. There were some advantages, of course. You could take ten of these bags a day and never become a junkie. You could be arrested with them and not be charged with possession of heroin. Thank God he hadn't shot it up, the Vim afterburn would have scorched his veins. What was he doing scoring off the street? He must be mad. He should have tried to get hold of Chilly Willy and sent him round to Loretta's. At least there were some traces of heroin in her little grease-proof packages.

Still, he wouldn't throw away this rubbish until he knew he could get something better. The cab had arrived at Sixth and C.

'Stop here,' said Patrick.

'I no wai' here,' shouted the driver in a sudden burst of vexation.

'Oh, well, fuck off then,' said Patrick, tossing a ten-dollar bill into the passenger seat and getting out of the cab. He slammed the door and stalked off towards Seventh Street. The taxi screeched away from the kerb. When it had gone, Patrick was conscious of a hush in which his footsteps seemed to ring loudly on the pavement. He was alone. But not for long. On the next corner, a group of about a dozen dealers were standing around outside the Bargain Grocery Store.

Patrick slowed down, and one of the men, spotting him first, detached himself from the group and sauntered across the street with a buoyant and muscular gait. An exceptionally tall black man, he wore a shiny red jacket.

'How you doing?' he asked Patrick. His face was completely smooth, his cheekbones high, and his wide eyes seemingly saturated with indolence.

'Fine,' said Patrick. 'How about you?'

'I'm good. What you looking for?'

'Can you take me to Loretta's?'

'Loretta,' said the black man lazily. 'Sure.'

Patrick was frustrated by his slowness and, feeling the book in his overcoat pocket, he imagined whipping it out like a pistol and gunning the dealer down with its ambitious first sentence, 'There is only one really serious philosophical problem: it is suicide.'

'How much you lookin' for?' asked the dealer, reaching nonchalantly behind his back.

'Just fifty dollars' worth,' said Patrick.

There was a sudden commotion on the other side of the street and he saw a half-familiar figure hobbling towards them in an agitated way.

'Don't stick him, don't stick him,' the new character shouted.

Patrick recognised him now: it was Chilly, clutching his trousers. He arrived, stumbling and out of breath. 'Don't stick him,' he repeated, 'he's my man.'

The tall black man smiled as if this was a truly hilarious incident. 'I was going to stick you,' he said, proudly showing Patrick a small knife. 'I didn't know yuz knew Chilly!'

'What a small world,' said Patrick wearily. He felt totally detached from the threat that this man claimed to represent, and impatient to get on with his business.

'That's right,' said the tall man, ever more ebullient. He offered his hand to Patrick, after removing the knife. 'My name's Mark,' he said. 'You ever need anything, ask for Mark.'

Patrick shook his hand and smiled at him faintly.

'Hello, Chilly,' he said.

'Where you been?' asked Chilly reproachfully.

'Oh, over to England. Let's go to Loretta's.'

Mark waved goodbye and lolloped back across the street. Patrick and Chilly headed downtown.

'Extraordinary man,' drawled Patrick. 'Does he always stab people when he first meets them?'

'He's a bad man,' said Chilly. 'You don't wanna hang around him. Why din't you ask for me?'

'I did,' Patrick lied, 'but of course he said you weren't around. I guess he wanted a free hand to stab me.'

'Yeah, he's a bad man,' repeated Chilly.

The two men turned the corner of Sixth Street and Chilly almost immediately led Patrick down a short flight of steps into the basement of a dela idated brownstone building. Patrick was quietly pleased that Chilly was taking him to Loretta's, instead of leaving him to wait on a street corner.

There was only one door in the basement, reinforced with steel and equipped with a brass flap and a small spyglass. Chilly rang the bell and soon after a voice called out suspiciously, 'Who's that?'

'It's Chilly.'

'How much you want?'

Patrick handed Chilly fifty dollars. Chilly counted the money, opened the brass flap and stuffed it inside. The flap retracted quickly and remained closed for what seemed like a long time.

'You got a bag for me?' asked Chilly, shifting from leg to leg.

'Of course,' replied Patrick magnificently, taking a ten-dollar bill out of his trouser pocket.

'Thanks, man.'

The flap reopened and Patrick clawed out the five little bags. Chilly got one for himself, and the two men left the building with a sense of achievement, counterbalanced by desire.

'Have you got any clean works?' asked Patrick.

'My ole lady got some. You wanna come back to my place?'

'Thanks,' said Patrick, flattered by these multiplying signs of trust and intimacy.

Chilly's place was a room on the second floor of a fire-gutted building. Its walls were blackened by smoke, and the unreliable staircase littered with empty matchbooks, liquor bottles, brown paper bags, heaps of cornered dust and balls of old hair. The room itself only contained one piece of furniture, a mustard-coloured armchair covered in burns, with a spring bursting from the centre of the seat, like an obscene tongue.

Mrs Chilly Willy – if that was her correct title, mused Patrick – was sitting on the arm of this chair when the two men came in. She was a large woman, more masculine in build than her skeletal husband.

'Hi, Chilly,' she said dozily, obviously further from withdrawal than he was.

'Hi,' he said, 'you know my man.'

'Hi, honey.'

'Hello,' beamed Patrick charmingly. 'Chilly said you might have a spare syringe.'

'I might,' she said playfully.

'Is it new?'

'Well, it ain't exactly noo, but I boiled it and everythin'.'

Patrick raised one eyebrow with deadly scepticism. 'Is it *very* blunt?' he asked.

She fished a bundle of loo paper out of her voluminous bra and carefully unwrapped the precious package. At its centre was a threateningly large syringe which a zoo-keeper would have hesitated to use on a sick elephant.

'That's not a needle, it's a bicycle pump,' Patrick protested, holding out his hand.

Intended for intramuscular use, the spike was worryingly thick, and when Patrick detached the green plastic head that held it he could not help noticing a ring of old blood inside. 'Oh, all right,' he said. 'How much do you want for it?'

'Gimme two bags,' urged Mrs Chilly, wrinkling up her nose endearingly.

It was an absurd price, but Patrick never argued about prices. He tossed two bags into her lap. If the stuff was any good he could always get more. Right now he had to shoot up. He asked Chilly to lend him a spoon and a cigarette filter. Since the light in the main room had failed, Chilly offered him the bathroom, a room without a bath in it, but with a black mark on the floor where there might once have been one. A naked bulb cast a dim yellow light on the insanely cracked basin and the seatless old loo.

Patrick trickled some water into the spoon and rested it at the back of the basin. Tearing open the three remaining packages, he wondered what sort of gear it was. Nobody could claim that Chilly looked well on a diet of Loretta's smack, but at least he wasn't dead. If Mr and Mrs Chilly were planning to shoot it up, there was no reason why he shouldn't. He could hear them whispering next door. Chilly was saying something about 'hurting' and was obviously trying to get the second bag out of his wife. Patrick emptied the three packets into the spoon and heated the solution, the flame from his lighter licking the already blackened underside of the spoon. As soon as it started to bubble, he cut off the heat and put the steaming liquid down again. He tore a thin strip off the cigarette filter, dropped it in the spoon, removed the spike from the syringe and sucked the liquid up through the filter. The barrel was so thick that the solution barely rose a quarter of an inch.

Dropping his overcoat and jacket on the floor, Patrick rolled up his sleeve and tried to make out his veins in the faint light which gave a hepatic glow to every object that was not already black. Luckily, his track marks formed brown and purple threads, as if his veins had been gunpowder trails burnt along his arm.

Patrick rolled the sleeve of his shirt tight around

his bicep and pumped his forearm up and down several times, clenching and unclenching his fist at the same time. He had good veins and, despite a certain shyness that resulted from his savage treatment of them, he was in a better position than many people whose daily search for a vein sometimes took up to an hour of exploratory digging.

He picked up the syringe and rested its point on the widest section of his track marks, slightly sideways to the scar. With such a long spike there was always a danger that it would go through the vein altogether and into the muscle on the other side, a painful experience, and so he approached the arm at a fairly low angle. At this crucial moment the syringe slipped from his hand and landed on a wet patch of the floor beside the loo. He could hardly believe what had happened. He felt vertiginous with horror and disappointment. There was a conspiracy against his having any fun today. He leant over, desperate with longing, and picked up the works from the damp patch. The spike wasn't bent. Thank God for that. Everything was all right. He quickly wiped the syringe on his trousers.

By now his heart was beating fast and he felt that visceral excitement, a combination of dread and desire, which always preceded a fix. He pushed the painfully blunt tip of the needle under his skin and thought he saw, miracle of miracles, a globule of blood shoot into the barrel. Not wanting to waste any time with such an unwieldy instrument, he put his thumb on the plunger and pushed it straight down.

He felt a violent and alarming swelling in his arm and recognised immediately that the spike had slipped out of his vein and he had squirted the solution under his skin.

'Shit,' he shouted.

Chilly came shuffling through. 'What's happening, man?'

'I missed,' said Patrick through clenched teeth, pushing the hand of his wounded arm up against his shoulder.

'Oh, man,' croaked Chilly sympathetically.

'Can I suggest you invest in a stronger lightbulb?' said Patrick pompously, holding his arm as if it had been broken.

'You shoulda used the flashlight,' said Chilly, scratching himself.

'Oh, thanks for telling me about it,' snapped Patrick.

'You wanna go back and score some more?' asked Chilly.

'No,' said Patrick curtly, putting his coat back on. 'I'm leaving.'

By the time he hit the street Patrick was wondering why he hadn't taken up Chilly's offer. 'Temper, temper,' he muttered sarcastically. He felt weary, but too frustrated to sleep. It was eleven-thirty; perhaps Pierre had woken up by now. He had better go back to the hotel.

Patrick hailed a cab.

'You live around here?' asked the driver.

'No, I was just trying to score,' Patrick sighed, posting the bags of Vim and barbs out of the window.

'You wanna score?'

'That's right,' sighed Patrick.

'Shee-eet, I know a better place than this.'

'Really?' said Patrick, all ears.

'Yeah, in the South Bronx.'

'Well, let's go.'

'All right,' laughed the driver.

At last a cab driver who was helpful. An experience like this might put him in a good mood. Perhaps he should write a letter to the Yellow Cab Company. 'Dear Sir,' murmured Patrick under his breath, 'I wish to commend in the highest possible terms the initiative and courtesy of your splendid young driver, Jefferson E. Parker. After a fruitless and, to be perfectly frank, infuriating expedition to Alphabet City, this knight errant, this, if I may put it thus, Jefferson Nightingale, rescued me from a very tiresome predicament, and took me to score in the South Bronx. If only more of your drivers displayed the same old-fashioned desire to serve. Yours, etc., Colonel Melrose.'

Patrick smiled. Everything was under control. He felt elated, almost frivolous. The Bronx was a bit of a worry for someone who had seen *Bronx Warriors* – a film of unremitting nastiness, not to be confused with the beautifully choreographed violence of the more simply, and more generically, named *Warriors* – but he felt invulnerable. People drew knives on him, but they could not touch him, and if they did he would not be there.

As the cab sped over a bridge Patrick had never crossed before, Jefferson turned his head slightly and said, 'We're gonna be in the Bronx soon.'

'I'll wait in the cab, shall I?' asked Patrick.

'You better lie on the floor,' laughed Jefferson, 'they don't like white people here.'

'On the floor?'

'Yeah, outa sight. If they see you, they gonna smash the windows. Shee-eet, I don't want my windows smashed.'

Jefferson stopped the taxi a few blocks beyond the bridge and Patrick sat down on the rubber floormat with his back against the door.

'How much you want?' asked Jefferson, leaning over the driver's seat.

'Oh, five bags. And get a couple for yourself,' said Patrick, handing over seventy dollars.

'Thanks,' said Jefferson. 'I'm gonna lock the doors now. You stay outa sight, right?'

'Right,' said Patrick, sliding down further and stretching out on the floor. The bolts of all the doors slithered into place. Patrick wriggled around for some time before curling up in a foetal position with his head on the central hump. After a few moments his hipbone was persecuting his liver and he felt hopelessly tangled up in the folds of his overcoat. He twisted around onto his front, rested his head in his hands and stared at the grooves in the floormat. There was quite a strong smell of oil down at this level. 'It gives you a whole new perspective on life,' said Patrick, in the voice of a television housewife.

It was intolerable. Everything was intolerable. He was always getting into these *situations*, always ending up with the losers, the dregs, the Chilly Willys of life. Even at school he had been sent every Tuesday and Thursday afternoons, when the other boys joined their teams and played their matches, to remote playing fields with every variety of sporting misfit: the pale and sensitive musicians, the hopelessly fat Greek boys, and the disaffected cigarette-smoking protesters who regarded physical exertion as hopelessly uncool. As a punishment for their unsporting natures, these boys were forced to make their way round an assault course. Mr Pitch, the overwrought pederast in charge of this unwholesome squad, quivered with excitement and malice as each boy crashed myopically, waddled feebly, or tried to beat the system by running around the wall at the beginning of the course. While the Greeks splattered into the mud, and the music scholars lost their spectacles, and the conscientious objectors made their cynical remarks, Mr Pitch rushed about screaming abuse at them about their 'privileged' lives and, if the opportunity arose, kicking them in the bottom.

What the hell was going on? Had Jefferson gone to fetch some friends so they could beat him up together, or was he simply being abandoned while Jefferson went to get stoned?

Yes, thought Patrick, shifting restlessly, he had hung out with nothing but failures. Living in Paris when he was nineteen, he had fallen in with Jim, an Australian heroin smuggler on the run, and Simon, a black American bank robber just out of prison. He could remember Jim saying, as he had searched for a vein among the thick orange hairs of his forearm, 'Australia's so beautiful in the spring, man. All the little lambs frisking about. You can tell they're just so happy to be alive.' He had pushed the plunger down with a whimsical expression on his face.

Simon had tried to rob a bank while he was withdrawing, but he had been forced to surrender to the police after they had fired several volleys at him. 'I didn't wanna look like no Swiss cheese,' he had explained.

Patrick heard the merciful sound of the locks opening again.

'I got it,' said Jefferson huskily.

'Goody,' said Patrick, sitting up.

Jefferson was happy and relaxed as he drove to the hotel. When he had snorted three of the bags Patrick could understand why. Here at last was a powder that contained a little heroin.

Jefferson and Patrick parted with the genuine

warmth of people who had exploited each other successfully.

Back in his hotel room, lying on the bed with his arms spread out, Patrick realised that if he took the other two bags and turned on the television he could probably fall asleep. Once he had taken heroin he could imagine being without it; when he was without it he could only imagine getting more. But just to see if all the evening's trouble had been completely unnecessary, he decided to call Pierre's number.

As the telephone rang he again wondered what kept him from suicide. Was it something as contemptible as sentimentality, or hope, or narcissism? No. It was really the desire to know what would happen next, despite the conviction that it was bound to be horrible: the narrative suspense of it all.

'Hallo?'

'Pierre!'

'Who iz this?'

'Patrick.'

'What do you want?'

'Can I come round?'

'Okay. How long?'

'Twenty minutes.'

'Okay.'

Patrick raised his fist in triumph and sprinted from the room.

CHAPTER SIX

'P ierre!'
'*Ça va?*' said Pierre, getting up from his
leather office chair. The parched yellow skin
of his face was stretched more tautly than ever over
the thin nose, high cheekbones and prominent jaw.
He shook hands with Patrick, fixing him with lantern
eyes.

The fetid atmosphere of the apartment struck
Patrick like the scent of a long-absent lover. The
stains of overturned coffee mugs still tattooed the
oatmeal carpet in the same places as before, and the
familiar pictures of severed heads floating on pieces
of jigsaw puzzle, lovingly executed by Pierre with a
fine ink pen, made Patrick smile.

'What a relief to see you again!' he exclaimed. 'I
can't tell you what a nightmare it is out there, scoring
off the streets.'

'You score off the street!' barked Pierre disapprov-
ingly. 'You fucking crazy!'

'But you were asleep.'

'You shoot with tap water?'

'Yes,' admitted Patrick guiltily.

'You crazy,' glared Pierre. 'Come in here, I show you.'

He walked through to his grimy and narrow kitchen. Opening the door of the big old-fashioned fridge, he took out a large jar of water.

'This is tap water,' said Pierre ominously, holding up the jar. 'I leave it one month and look . . .' He pointed to a diffuse brown sediment at the bottom of the jar. 'Rust,' he said, 'it's a fucking killer! I have one friend who shoot with tap water and the rust get in his bloodstream and his heart . . .' Pierre chopped the air with his hand and said, '*Tak*: it stop.'

'That's appalling,' murmured Patrick, wondering when they were going to do business.

'The water come from the mountains,' said Pierre, sitting down in his swivel chair and sucking water from a glass into an enviably slim syringe, 'but the pipes are full of rust.'

'I'm lucky to be alive,' said Patrick without conviction. 'It's nothing but mineral water from now on, I promise.'

'It's the City,' said Pierre darkly; 'they keep the money for new pipes. They kill my friend. What do you want?' he added, opening a package and piling some white powder into a spoon with the corner of a razor blade.

'Um . . . a gram of smack,' said Patrick casually, 'and seven grams of coke.'

'The smack is six hundred. The coke I make you

82

a price: one hundred a gram instead of one-twenty. Total: thirteen hundred dollar.'

Patrick slipped the orange envelope out of his pocket while Pierre piled another white powder into the spoon and stirred it, frowning like a child pretending to make cement.

Was that nine or ten? Patrick started counting again. When he reached thirteen he tapped the notes together like a shuffled deck of cards and tossed them over to Pierre's side of the mirror where they fanned out extravagantly. Pierre wound a length of rubber around his bicep and gripped it in his teeth. Patrick was pleased to see that he still had the use of the volcano cone in the hollow of his arm.

Pierre's pupils dilated for a moment and then contracted again, like the feeding mouth of a sea anemone.

'Okay,' he croaked, trying to give the impression that nothing had happened, but sounding subdued by pleasure, 'I give you what you want.' He refilled the syringe and squirted the contents into a second pinkish glass of water.

Patrick wiped his clammy hands on his trousers. Only the need to make one more tricky negotiation contained his heart-exploding impatience.

'Do you have any spare syringes?' he asked.

Pierre could be very awkward about syringes. Their value varied wildly according to how many he had left, and although he was generally helpful to Patrick when he had spent over a thousand dollars, there was always the danger that he would lapse into an indignant lecture on his presumption.

'I give you two,' said Pierre with delinquent generosity.

'Two!' exclaimed Patrick as if he had just witnessed a medieval relic waving from behind its glass case.

Pierre took out a pair of pale green scales and measured the quantities Patrick had requested, giving him individual gram packets so that he could keep track of his coke consumption.

'Ever thoughtful, ever kind,' murmured Patrick.

The two precious syringes followed across the dusty mirror.

'I get you some water,' said Pierre.

Perhaps he had put more heroin than usual in the speedball. How else could one explain this unaccustomed benevolence?

'Thanks,' said Patrick, slipping hastily out of his overcoat and jacket and rolling up his shirt sleeve. Jesus! There was a black bulge in his skin where he had missed the vein round at Chilly's. He'd better not let Pierre see this sign of his incompetence and desperation. Pierre was such a moral man. Patrick let the sleeve flop down, undid the gold cufflink of his right sleeve and rolled that up instead. Fixing was the one activity in which he had become truly ambidextrous. Pierre came back with one full and one empty glass, and a spoon.

Patrick unfolded one of the packets of coke. The shiny white paper was imprinted with a pale blue polar bear. Unlike Pierre he preferred to take coke on its own until the tension and fear were unbearable, then he would send in the Praetorian Guard of heroin to save the day from insanity and defeat. He held the packet in a funnel and tapped it gently. Small grains of powder slipped down the narrow valley of paper and tumbled into the spoon. Not too much for the first fix. Not too little either. Nothing was more intolerable than a dissipated, watery rush. He carried on tapping.

'How are you?' asked Pierre, so rapidly that the question seemed like one word.

'Well, my father died the other day and so . . .' Patrick was not sure what to say. He looked at the packet, gave it one more decisive tap, and another flurry of powder joined the small heap already in the spoon. 'And so I'm a little confused at the moment,' he concluded.

'How was he, your father?'

'He was a kitten,' Patrick intoned rhapsodically. 'And he had such artistic hands.' For a moment the water went syrupy and then it dissolved into a clear solution. 'He could have been prime minister,' he added.

'He was in politic?' asked Pierre, narrowing his eyes.

'No, no,' Patrick replied, 'it was a sort of joke. In his world – a world of pure imagination – it was better if a person "could have been" prime minister than if he *was* prime minister: that would have shown vulgar ambition.' There was a faint metallic ringing as he directed the jet of water from his syringe against the side of the spoon.

'*Tu regrettes qu'il est mort*?' asked Pierre shrewdly.

'*Non, absolument pas, je regrette qu'il ait vécu.*'

'*Mais sans lui*, you would not exist.'

'One shouldn't be egotistical about these things,' said Patrick with a smile.

His right arm was relatively unscathed. A few bruises the colour of tobacco stains yellowed his lower forearm, and faded pink puncture marks clustered around the bull's-eye of his principal vein. He raised the needle and allowed a couple of drops to dribble from its eye. His stomach made a rumbling sound and he felt as nervous and excited as a twelve-year-old in the back of a darkened cinema stretching his arm around a girl's shoulders for the first time.

He aimed the needle at the centre of the existing puncture marks and pushed it almost painlessly under his skin. A thread of blood burst into the barrel and curled around, a private mushroom cloud, luminously red in the clear bitter water. Thank God he had found a vein. His heart rate increased, like the drumbeat of a galley rowing into battle. Holding the barrel firmly between his fingers he pushed the plunger down slowly. Like a film in reverse the blood shot back through the needle towards its source.

Before he felt its effects he smelt the heartbreaking fragrance of the cocaine, and then a few seconds afterwards, in a time-lapse frenzy, its cold geometric flowers broke out everywhere and carpeted the surface of his inner vision. Nothing could ever be as pleasurable as this. He clumsily drew back the plunger, filled the barrel with blood and injected himself a second time. Drunk with pleasure, choking with love, he lurched forward and put the syringe down heavily on the mirror. He would have to flush it out before the blood coagulated, but he couldn't do it straight away. The sensation was too strong. Sound was twisted and amplified until it whistled like the engine of a landing jet.

Patrick sat back and closed his eyes, his lips thrust out like a child waiting for a kiss. Sweat had already broken out high on his forehead, and his armpits dripped every few seconds like defective taps.

Pierre knew exactly what state Patrick was in and disapproved strongly of his unbalanced approach, and the irresponsible way he had put his syringe down without flushing it out. He picked it up and filled it with water so that the mechanism didn't block. Sensing a movement, Patrick opened his eyes and whispered, 'Thank you.'

'You should take smack at the same time,' said Pierre reproachfully; 'it's medicine, man, medicine.'

'I like the rush.'

'But you take too much, you lose control.'

Patrick sat up and looked at Pierre intently. 'I never lose control,' he said, 'I just test its limits.'

'Bullshit,' said Pierre, unimpressed.

'Of course you're right,' smiled Patrick. 'But you

know what it's like trying to stay on the edge without falling off it,' he said, appealing to their traditional solidarity.

'I know what it's like,' screeched Pierre, his eyes incandescent with passion. 'For eight years I thought I was an egg, but I had total control, *contrôle total.*'

'I remember,' said Patrick soothingly.

The rush was over, and like a surfer who shoots out of a tube of furling, glistening sea only to peter out and fall among the breaking waves, his thoughts began to scatter before the onset of boundless unease. Only a few minutes after the fix he felt a harrowing nostalgia for the dangerous exhilaration which was already dying out. As if his wings had melted in that burst of light, he felt himself falling towards a sea of unbearable disappointment, and it was this that made him pick up the syringe, finish flushing it out and, despite his shaking hands, begin to prepare another fix.

'Do you think the measure of a perversion is its need to be repeated, its inability to be satisfied?' he asked Pierre. 'I wish my father were around to answer that question,' he added piously.

'Why? He was a junkie?'

'No, no . . .' said Patrick. He wanted to say, 'it was a kind of joke' again, but resisted. 'What sort of man was *your* father?' he asked hastily, in case Pierre followed up his remark.

'He was a *fonctionnaire*,' said Pierre contemptuously, '*Métro, boulot, dodo.* His happiest days were his *service militaire*, and the proudest moment of his life was when the Minister congratulated him for saying nothing. Can you imagine? Each time someone visited the house, which was not often, my father would tell the same story.' Pierre straightened his back, smiled complacently and wagged his finger. ' "*Et Monsieur le Ministre m'a dit, Vous avez eu raison de ne rien dire.*" When he told that story I used to run from the room. It fill me with disgust, *j'avais un dégoût total*.'

'And your mother?' said Patrick, pleased to have got Pierre off his own parental case.

'What is a woman who is not maternal?' snapped Pierre. 'A piece of furniture with breasts!'

'Quite,' said Patrick, sucking a new solution into his syringe. As a concession to Pierre's medical advice, he had decided to take some heroin rather than further delay the onset of serenity with another chilling shot of cocaine.

'You have to leave all that behind,' said Pierre. 'Parents, all that shit. You have to invent yourself again to become an individual.'

'Right on,' said Patrick, knowing it was best not to argue with Pierre's theories.

'The Americans, they talk all the time about individuality, but they don't have an idea unless everybody else is having the same idea at the same time. My American customers, they always fuck me about to show they are individuals, but they always do it in exactly the same way. Now I have no American customers.'

'People think they are individuals because they use the word "I" so often,' Patrick commented.

'When I died in the hospital,' said Pierre, *j'avais une conscience sans limites*. I knew everything, man, literally *everything*. After that I cannot take seriously the *sociologues et psychologues* who say you are "schizoid" or "paranoid", or "social class 2" or "social class 3". These people know nothing. They think they know about the human mind, but they know nothing, *absolument rien*.' Pierre glared vehemently at Patrick. 'It's like they put moles in charge of the space programme,' he sneered.

Patrick laughed drily. He had stopped listening to Pierre and started searching for a vein. When he saw a poppy of blood light up the barrel, he administered the injection, and pulled out the syringe, flushing it out efficiently this time.

He was amazed by the strength and smoothness of the heroin. His blood became as heavy as a sack of coins and he sank down appreciatively into his body, resolved again into a single substance after the catapulting exile of the cocaine.

'Exactly,' he whispered, 'like moles . . . God, this is good smack.' He closed his eyelids lingeringly.

'It's pure,' said Pierre. '*Fais attention, c'est très fort.*'

'Mm, I can tell.'

'It's medicine, man, medicine,' Pierre reiterated.

'Well, I'm completely cured,' whispered Patrick

with a private smile. Everything was going to be all right. A coal fire on a stormy night, rain that could not touch him beating against the window-pane. Streams made of smoke, and smoke that formed into shining pools. Thoughts shimmering on the borders of a languorous hallucination.

He scratched his nose and reopened his eyes. Yes, with the firm base provided by the heroin, he could play high notes of cocaine all night without cracking altogether.

But he'd have to be alone for that. With good drugs, solitude was not just bearable, it was indispensable. 'It's much more subtle than Persian smack,' he croaked. 'A gentle sustained curve . . . like a, like a polished tortoise shell.' He closed his eyes again.

'It's the strongest smack in the world,' said Pierre simply.

'Ya,' drawled Patrick, 'it's such a bore, one can hardly ever get it in England.'

'You should come and live here.'

'Good idea,' said Patrick amiably. 'By the way, what's the time?'

'One-forty-seven.'

'Gosh, I'd better go to bed,' said Patrick, putting the syringes carefully into his inside pocket. 'It's been lovely seeing you again. I'll be in touch very soon.

'Okay,' said Pierre. 'I'm awake tonight, tomorrow, and tomorrow night.'

'Perfect,' said Patrick nodding.

He put on his jacket and overcoat. Pierre got up,

undid the four security locks, opened the door and let him out.

CHAPTER SEVEN

Patrick slumped back in the chair. The tension was deleted from his chest. For a moment he fell quiet. But soon a new character installed itself in his body, forcing his shoulders back and his stomach out, and launching him into another bout of compulsive mimicry.

The Fat Man (pushing back the chair to accommodate his huge stomach): 'I feel compelled to speak, sir, indeed I do. Compelled, sir, is a mild description of the obligation under which I am placed in this matter. My story is a simple one, the story of a man who loved not wisely but too well.' (Wipes a tear from the corner of his eye.) 'A man who ate not from greed, but from passion. Eating, sir – I do not attempt to disguise it – has been my life. Couched in the ruins of this old body are the traces of some of the most exquisite dishes ever cooked. When horses have collapsed beneath my bulk, their legs shattered or their lungs flooded with their own blood, or I have been forced to renounce the fruitless struggle to intervene between the seat and the steering wheel of

93

a motor car, I have consoled myself with the reflection that my weight has been won, and not merely "put on". Naturally, I have dined in Les Bains and Les Baux, but I have also dined in Quito and Khartoum. And when the ferocious Yanomani offered me a dish of human flesh, I did not allow prudishness to prevent me from requesting a third helping. Indeed I did not, sir.' (Smiles wistfully.)

Nanny (huffing and puffing): 'Human flesh indeed! Whatever next? You always were a strange boy.'

'Oh, shut up,' screamed Patrick silently, as he paced across the faded green carpet and turned around abruptly.

Gary (raising his eyes to heaven with a charming little sigh): 'My name's Gary, I'll be your waiter tonight. Today's specials include a Dish of Human Flesh, and a sodium-free Frisson of Colombian Cocaine nestling on a bed of "Wild Baby" Chinese White Heroin.'

Pete Bloke: 'Haven't you got any Hovis, then?'

Mrs Bloke: 'Yeah, we want Hovis.'

Hovis Voice-over (theme music from *Coronation Street*): 'It were grand when I were young. I'd go round t' dealer's, buy 'alf an ounce a' coke and four grams a' smack, order round a case a' champagne from Berry Bros, take wench out ta Mirabelle, and still 'ave change from a farthing. Them were the days.'

He was dangerously out of control. Every thought or hint of a thought took on a personality stronger than his own. 'Please, please, please make it stop,' muttered Patrick, getting up and pacing about the room.

Mocking echo: 'Please, please, please make it stop.'

Nanny: 'I know about the aristocracy and their filthy ways.'

Humpo Languid (laughing disarmingly): 'What filthy ways, Nanny?'

Nanny: 'Oh, no, you won't find Nanny telling tales out of school. My lips are sealed. Whatever would Lady Deadwood think? Rolling stones gather no moss. You mark my words. You always were a strange boy.'

Mrs Garsington: 'Who is in charge here? I wish to speak to the manager immediately.'

Dr McCoy: 'It's life, Jim, but not as we know it.'

Captain Kirk (flicking open his communicator): 'Beam us up, Scottie.'

Patrick opened the packet of heroin and, in too much of a hurry to make another fix, simply tipped some of it onto the glass which protected the surface of the table.

Indignant Eric (knowingly): 'Oh, typical, faced with a problem: take more heroin. Basically, the ultimate self-perpetuating system.'

Pulling a banknote out of his pocket, Patrick sat down and stooped over the table.

Captain Languid: 'I say, Sergeant, shut those fellows up, will you?'

Sergeant: 'Don't worry, sir, we'll bring them

95

under control. They're nothing but a bunch of fuzzy-wuzzies, black-souled bastards, sir, never seen a Gatling in their miserable, godless lives, sir.'

Captain Languid: 'Well done, Sergeant.'

Patrick sniffed up the powder, threw his head back, and inhaled deeply through his nose.

Sergeant: 'Allow me to take the brunt of the impact, sir.' (Groans, a spear lodged in his chest.)

Captain Languid: 'Oh, thank you . . . um . . .'

Sergeant: 'Wilson, sir.'

Captain Languid: 'Yes, of course. Well done, Wilson.'

Sergeant: 'Only wish I could do the same again, sir. But I'm sorry to say I've been fatally wounded, sir.'

Captain Languid: 'Oh, dear. Well, get that wound seen to, Sergeant.'

Sergeant: 'Thank you, sir, very kind of you. What a wonderful gentleman!'

Captain Languid: 'And if the worst should happen, I'm sure we can get you some sort of posthumous gong. My uncle is the chap in charge of that sort of thing.'

Sergeant (sitting up and saluting, shouts): 'Sir!' (Sinking back.) 'It'll mean a lot to Mrs Wilson and the toddlers, poor little fatherless mites.' (Groans.) 'What . . . a . . . wonderful gentleman.'

George the Barman (polishing a glass meditatively): 'Oh, yes, that Captain Languid, I remember him well. Used to come in here and always ask for nine oysters. Not half a dozen or a dozen, but nine. What a gentleman! They don't make 'em like that any more. I remember The Fat Man as well. Oh yes, not likely to forget him. We couldn't have him in the bar towards the end, literally couldn't fit him in. What a gentleman, though! One of the old school, didn't go in for all this dieting, dear me, no.'

The Fat Man (standing in an especially enlarged dock at the Old Bailey): 'It has indeed been my misfortune, sir, to live in an age of diets and regimens.' (Wipes a tear from the corner of his eye.) 'They call me The Fat Man, and I am fat enough to flatter myself that the epithet requires no explanation. I stand accused of unnatural appetites and an unnatural degree of appetite. Can I be blamed, sir, if I have filled my cup to the brim, if I have piled the plate of my life high with the *Moules au Menthe Fraîches* of experience (a dish to wake the dead, sir, a dish to charm a king!)? I have not been one of those timid waifs of modern life, I have not been a poor guest at the Feast. Dead men, sir, do not accept the challenge of the *Menu Gastronomique* at the Lapin Vert when they have scarcely swallowed the last mouthful of the *Petit Déjeuner Médiéval* at the Château de l'Enterrement. They do not then have themselves driven by ambulance, (the natural transport of the *Bon Viveur*, sir, the carriage of a king!) to the Sac d'Argent to launch themselves with grim abandon down the Cresta Run of their Carte Royale.' (The violinist from the Café Florian plays in the background.) 'My last days, last days, sir, for I fear that my liver – oh, it has done me valiant service, but now it has grown tired and I have grown tired too; but enough of that – my last days have been clouded with calumny.' (Sound of muffled sobbing in the court.) 'But I do not regret the course, or rather the courses,' (sad little laugh) 'I have taken in life, indeed I don't.' (Gathers all his dignity.) 'I have eaten, and I have eaten bravely.'

Judge (with thunderous indignation): 'This case is dismissed. It is a grave miscarriage of justice that it was ever brought to trial and, in recognition of that fact, the court awards The Fat Man a dinner for one at the Pig and Whistle.'

Contented Populace: 'Hooray! Hooray!'

Patrick felt limitless dread. The rotten floorboards of his thoughts gave way one after another until the ground itself seemed no fitter than sodden paper to catch his fall. Maybe it would never stop. 'I'm so tired, so tired,' he said, sitting down on the edge of the bed, but immediately getting up again.

Mocking Echo: 'I'm so tired, I'm so tired.'

Greta Garbo (screaming hysterically): 'I don't want to be alone. I'm sick of being alone.'

Patrick slid down the wall. 'I'm so fucking tired,' he wailed.

Mrs Mop: 'You have a nice fix of coke, dear, perk yourself up a bit.'

Dr Death (taking out a syringe): 'I have just the

thing for you. We always use it in cases of bereavement.'

Cleopatra: 'Oh, yes.' (Pouting girlishly.) 'My bluest veins to kiss.'

Mrs Mop: 'Go on, dear, do yourself a favour.'

Cleopatra (hoarsely): 'Go on, you bastard, fuck me.'

This time Patrick had to use his tie. He wound it around his bicep several times and gripped it in his teeth, baring his gums like a snarling dog.

Gift o' the Gab O'Connor (draining a glass of Jameson's): 'She took to the leech with rowdy Saxon abandon crying, "I've always wanted to be in two places at once." '

Courtier (excitedly): 'A hit, a palpable hit.'

Captain Kirk: 'Warp factor ten, Mr Sulu.'

Attila the Hun (basso profundo): 'I play football with the heads of my enemies. I ride under triumphal arches, my horse's hooves striking sparks from the cobblestones, the slaves of Rome strewing flowers in my path.'

Patrick fell off the chair and curled up on the floor. The brutality of the rush left him winded and amazed. He shook from the violence of his own heartbeat, like a man cowering under the spinning blades of a helicopter. His limbs were paralysed with tension and he imagined his veins, as thin and brittle as the stems of champagne glasses, snapping if he tried to unbend his arms. Without heroin he would die of a heart attack. 'Just fuck off, the lot of you,' he murmured.

Honest John (shaking his head): 'What a vicious bastard, eh, that Attila. Dear, oh dear. "Wot you staring at?" he said. "Nothing," I said. "Well, don't fucking do it, all right?" he said.' (Shakes his head.) 'Vicious!'

Nanny: 'Nanny says if you don't stop talking in silly voices, the wind will change, and you won't be able to stop.'

Boy (desperately): 'But I want to stop, Nanny.'

Nanny: ' "I want" gets nowhere.'

Sergeant: 'Get a grip on yourself, laddie.' (Screaming): 'Quick march! Left, right. Left, right.'

Patrick's legs slid back and forth across the carpet, like a tipped-over wind-up doll.

Short Notice in *The Times*' Death Column: 'MEL-ROSE. On May 25, peacefully, after a happy day in the Pierre Hotel. Patrick, aged 22, loving son of David and Eleanor, will be sadly missed by Attila the Hun, Mrs Mop, Indignant Eric, and his many friends, too numerous to enumerate.'

Gift o' the Gab O'Connor: 'A poor unfortunate soul. If he was not twitching like the severed leg of a galvanised frog, it was only because the mood lay heavy on him, like pennies on the eyelids of the dead.' (Drains a tumbler of Jameson's.)

Nanny (older now, her memory no longer what it was): 'I can't get used to it, he was such a lovely little boy. Always called him "my precious pet", I remember. Always said, "Don't forget that Nanny loves you." '

Gift o' the Gab O'Connor (tears rolling down his cheeks): 'And his poor unfortunate arms fit to make a strong man weep. Covered in wounds they were, like the mouths of hungry goldfish crying out for the only thing that would purchase a little peace for his poor troubled heart.' (Drains a tumbler of Jameson's.)

Captain Languid: 'He was the sort of chap who stayed in his room a good deal. Nothing wrong with that, of course, except that he paced about the whole time. As I like to say, if one's going to be idle, one should be thoroughly idle.' (Smiles charmingly.)

Gift o' the Gab O'Connor (drinking straight from the bottle now, knee deep in tears, his speech grown more slurred): 'And he was troubled in his mind also. Maybe it was the worry of the freedom killed him? In every situation – and he was always getting himself into situations – he saw the choices stretching out crazily, like the broken blood-vessels of tired eyes. And with every action he heard the death cry of all the things he had not done. And he saw the chance to get the vertigo, even in a sky-catching puddle, or the gleaming of a drain on the corner of Little Britain Street. Maddened he was by the terror of forgetting and losing the trail of who he was, and turning in circles, like a foxy bloody foxhound in the middle of the bloody wood.'

Honest John: 'What a prannit, eh? Never did an

honest day's work in his life. When did you ever see him help an old lady across the road, or buy a bag of sweets for some deprived kiddies? Never. You gotta be honest.'

The Fat Man: 'He was a man, sir, who did not eat enough, a man who picked at his food, who turned from the cornucopia to the pharmacopoeia of life. In short, sir, the worst kind of scoundrel.'

Gift o' the Gab O'Connor (occasionally surfacing above a lake of tears): 'And the sight of him . . .' (glug, glug, glug) '. . . those torn lips that had never learned to love . . .' (glug, glug, glug) '. . . Those lips that had spoken wild and bitter words . . .' (glug, glug, glug) '. . . torn open by the fury of it, and the knowledge that death was upon him' (glug).

Debbie (stammering): 'I wonder what I'm meant to say?'

Kay: 'I saw him the day it happened.'

'Let me not go mad,' shouted Patrick in a voice that started like his own, but became more like John Gielgud's with the last two words.

The Vicar (looking down soothingly from the pulpit): 'Some of us remember David Melrose as a paedophile, an alcoholic, a liar, a rapist, a sadist, and a "thoroughly nasty piece of work". But, you know, in a situation like that, what Christ asks us to say, and what he would have said himself in his own words is' (pausing) ' "But that's not the whole story, is it?" '

Honest John: 'Yes it is.'

The Vicar: 'And that "whole story" idea is one of the most exciting things about Christianity. When we read a book by one of our favourite authors, be he Richard Bach or Peter Mayle, we don't just want to know that it's about a very special seagull, or that it's set in the lovely *campagne*, to use a French word, of Provence; we want the satisfaction of reading all the way to the end.'

Honest John: 'Speak for yourself.'

The Vicar: 'And in very much the same spirit, when we make judgements about other people (and which one of us doesn't?) we have to make sure that we have the "whole story" spread out before us.'

Attila the Hun (basso profundo): 'Die, Christian dog!' (Decapitates the Vicar.)

Vicar's severed head (pausing thoughtfully): 'You know, the other day, my young granddaughter came to me and said, "Grandfather, I *like* Christianity." And I said to her (thoroughly puzzled), "Why?" And do you know what she said?'

Honest John: 'Of course we don't, you prannit.'

Vicar's severed head: 'She said, "Because it's such a comfort." ' (Pauses, and then more slowly and emphatically): ' "Because it's such a comfort." '

Patrick opened his eyes and uncurled slowly on the floor. The television stared at him accusingly. Perhaps it could save him or distract him from his own involuntary performance.

Television (snivelling and shivering): 'Turn me on, man. Gimme a turn-on.'

Mr President: 'Ask not what your television can do for you, but what you can do for your television.'

Ecstatic Populace: 'Hooray! Hooray!'

Mr President: 'We shall pay any price, bear any burden, meet any hardship . . .'

Von Trapp Family Singers (ecstatically): 'Climb every mountain!'

Mr President: '. . . support any friend, oppose any foe, to assure the survival and success of television.'

Ecstatic Populace: 'Hooray! Hooray!'

Mr President: 'Let the word go forth from this time and place, that the torch has passed to a new generation of Americans – born in this century, tempered by war, disciplined by a hard and bitter peace, proud of our ancient heritage and unwilling to do anything except watch television.'

'Yes, yes, yes,' thought Patrick, crawling across the floor, 'television.'

Television (shifting restlessly from wheel to wheel): 'Gimme a turn on, man, I gotta have it.'

Viewer (coolly): 'What you got for me?'

Television (ingratiatingly): 'I got *The Million-Dollar Movie. The Billion-Dollar Man. The Trillion-Dollar Quiz Show.*'

Viewer: 'Yeahyeahyeah, but wot you got *now*?'

Television (guiltily): 'A still of the American flag, and some weirdo in a pale blue nylon suit talkin' about the end of the world. The Farming Report should be comin' up real soon.'

Viewer: 'Okay, I guess I'll take the flag. But don't

push me' (getting out a revolver) 'or I'll blow your fuckin' screen out.'

Television: 'Okay, man, just keep cool, okay? The reception isn't too great, but it's a *real* good shot of the flag. I personally guarantee that.'

Patrick switched off the television. When would this dreadful night come to an end? Clambering onto the bed, he collapsed, closed his eyes, and listened intently to the silence.

Ron Zak (his eyes closed, smiling benignly): 'I want you to listen to that silence. Can you hear it?' (Pause.) 'Become part of that silence. That silence is your inner voice.'

Honest John: 'Oh, dear, it's not over yet, eh? Who's this Ron Zak, then? Sounds like a bit of a prannit, to be honest.'

Ron Zak: 'Are you all one with that silence?'

Students: 'We are one with the silence, Ron.'

Ron Zak: 'Good.' (Long pause.) 'Now I want you to use the Visualisation Technique you learned last week to picture a pagoda – that's kind of a Chinese beach house, only in the hills.' (Pause.) 'Good. It's very beautiful, isn't it?'

Students: 'Gee, Ron, it's so neat.'

Ron Zak: 'It's got a beautiful golden roof, and a network of bubbling round pools in the garden. Climb into one of those pools – mm, it feels good – and allow the gatekeepers to wash your body and bring you fresh new robes made of silk and other prestigious fabrics. They feel good, don't they?'

Students: 'Oh, yes, they feel great.'

Ron Zak: 'Good. Now I want you to go into the pagoda.' (Pause.) 'There's somebody in there, isn't there?'

Students: 'Yes, it is the Guide we learned about the week before last.'

Ron Zak (a little irritably): 'No, the Guide is in another room.' (Pause.) 'It's your mom and dad.'

Students (in startled recognition): 'Mom? Dad?'

Ron Zak: 'Now I want you to go over to your mom and say, "Mom, I *really* love you." '

Students: 'Mom, I *really* love you.'

Ron Zak: 'Now I want you to embrace her.' (Pause.) 'It feels good, doesn't it?'

Students (they scream, faint, write cheques, embrace each other, burst into tears, and punch pillows): 'It feels so good!'

Ron Zak: 'Now I want you to go over to Dad and say, "You, on the other hand, I cannot forgive." '

Students: 'You, on the other hand, I cannot forgive.'

Ron Zak: 'Take out a revolver and shoot his fuckin' brains out. Bang. Bang. Bang. Bang.'

Students: 'Bang. Bang. Bang. Bang.'

Koenig Spook (terrible creaking of armour): 'Omlet! Ich bin thine Popospook!'

'Oh, for fuck's sake,' shouted Patrick, sitting up and slapping himself across the face, 'stop thinking about it.'

Mocking Echo: 'Stop thinking about it.'

106

Patrick sat down at the table and picked up the packet of coke. He tapped the packet and an unusually large rock fell into the spoon. Bringing a jet of water down on the cocaine, he heard a silvery ringing where it struck the side of the spoon. The powder flooded and dissolved.

His veins were beginning to shrink from the savage onslaught of the evening but one vein, lower down the forearm, still showed without encouragement. Thick and blue, it snaked its way towards his wrist. The skin was tougher there, and it hurt to break beneath it.

Nanny (singing dreamily to her veins): 'Come out, come out, wherever you are!'

A thread of blood appeared in the barrel.

Cleopatra (gasping): 'Oh, yes, yes, yes, yes, yes.'

Attila the Hun (viciously, through clenched teeth): 'No prisoners!'

Patrick fainted and sank back onto the floor, feeling as if his body had suddenly been filled with wet cement. There was silence as he looked down on his body from the ceiling.

Pierre: 'Look at your body, man, it's fucking rubbish. *Tu as une conscience totale*. No *limites*.' (Patrick's body accelerates very rapidly. Space turns from blue to dark blue, and from dark blue to black. The clouds are like the pieces of a jigsaw puzzle. Patrick looks down and sees, far below him, the window of his hotel room. Inside the room is a thin white beach surrounded by an intensely blue sea. On the beach children are burying Patrick's body in the sand. Only the head is showing. He thinks he can break the case of sand with a simple movement, but he realises his mistake when one of the children empties a bucket of wet concrete in his face. He tries to wipe the concrete from his mouth and eyes, but his arms are trapped in a concrete tomb.)

'Jennifer's Diary': 'Patrick Melrose's graveside appeared to be unattended as the coffin was lowered, somewhat roughly, into the ground. However, all was not lost, and in the nick of time, that ever-popular, gracious, enchanting, indefatigable couple, Mr and Mrs Chilly Willy, the Alphabet City junkies, on a rare visit uptown, shuffled attractively onto the scene. "Don't sink him, don't sink him, he's my man," cried the inconsolable Chilly Willy. "Where I gonna git a dime bag now?" he wailed. "Did he leave me anything in his will?" asked his grief-stricken wife, who wore a cleverly-designed, affordable dress in a superbly colourful floral fabric. Among those who did not attend, claiming that they had never heard of the deceased, were Sir Veridian Gravalaux-Gravalax, Marshal of the Island Kennels, and his cousin the very attractive Miss Rowena Keats-Shelley.'

Honest John: 'I don't think he's going to survive this one, to be honest.'

Indignant Eric (shaking his head incredulously): 'What amazes me is that people think they can come along and, eh, casually, eh, bury people alive.'

Mrs Chronos (carrying a huge hourglass, and wearing a tattered old ballgown): 'Well, I must say, it's nice to be wanted! Not a single part since the fourth act of *The Winter's Tale*' (warmly). 'A play by Bill Shakespeare, of course – a lovely man, by the way, and a close personal friend. As the centuries slipped past I thought, "That's right, just ignore me, I know when I'm not wanted." ' (Folds her arms and nods.) 'People think of me as a character actor, but if there's one thing I can't stand, it's being type-cast. Anyway,' (little sigh) 'I suppose it's time to say my lines.' (Pulling a face.) 'Frankly, I find them a little bit old-fashioned. People don't seem to appreciate that I'm a modern girl.' (Coy laugh.) 'I just want to say one more thing,' (serious now) 'and that's a big "thank you" to all my fans. You kept me going during the lonely years. Thank you for the sonnets, and the letters and the conversations, they mean a lot, they really do. Think of me sometimes, darlings, when your gums go black, and you can't remember someone's name.' (Blows kisses to the audience. Then composes herself, smooths the folds of her dress and walks front stage.)

> 'Since his death cannot be mended,
> All our revels now are ended.
> Think not harshly of our play
> But come again another day.'

Attila the Hun (punches the lid off his coffin, making a sound of growling, snarling hissing fury,

like a leopard being baited through the bars of a cage):
'Raaaarrrrrghh!'

Patrick shot bolt upright and banged his head on
the leg of the chair. 'Shit, wank, fuck, blast,' he said
in his own voice at last.

CHAPTER EIGHT

Patrick lay on the bed like a dead thing. He had parted the curtains for a moment and seen the sun rising over the East River, and it had filled him with loathing and self-reproach.

The sun shone, having no alternative, on the nothing new. That was another first sentence.

Other people's words drifted through his mind. Tumbleweed riding through a desert. Had he already thought that? Had he already said it? He felt bloated and empty at the same time.

Traces of the night's possession surfaced now and again in the slowly simmering scum of his thoughts, and the experience of being so thoroughly and often displaced left him bruised and lonely. Besides, he had almost killed himself.

'Let's not go over that again,' he murmured, like a beleaguered lover who is never allowed to forget an indiscretion.

He winced as he stretched out his aching and sticky arm to check the time on the bedside clock. Five-forty-five. He could order a selection of cold meats

111

or a plate of smoked salmon straight away, but it would be another three-quarters of an hour before he could organise that brief moment of affirmation when a trolley rattling with wholesome breakfast food was wheeled into the room.

Then the fruit juice would sweat and separate under its cardboard cap; the bacon and egg, too intimidatingly carnal after all, would grow cold and begin to smell, and the single rose, in its narrow glass vase, would drop a petal on the white table-cloth, while he gulped down some sugary tea and continued to ingest the ethereal food of his syringe.

After a sleepless night, he always spent the hours from five-thirty to eight cowering from the gathering roar of life. In London, when the pasty light of dawn had stained the ceiling above the curtain-pole, he would listen with vampirish panic to the squealing and rumbling of distant juggernauts, and then to the nearby whining of a milkcart, and eventually to the slamming doors of cars bearing children to school, or real men to work in factories and banks.

It was nearly eleven o'clock in England. He could kill the time until breakfast with a few telephone calls. He would ring Johnny Hall, who was bound to sympathise with his state of mind.

But first he had to have a little fix to keep him going. Just as he could only contemplate giving up heroin when he had already taken some, so he could only recover from the ravages of cocaine by taking more.

112

After a fix of a moderation that impressed him almost as much as it bored him, Patrick propped up some pillows and installed himself comfortably beside the phone.

'Johnny?'

'Yup.' There was a strained whisper at the other end of the line.

'It's Patrick.'

'What time is it?'

'Eleven.'

'I've only had three hours' sleep in that case.'

'Do you want me to ring back?'

'No, the damage is already done. How are you?'

'Oh, fine. I've had a rather heavy night.'

'Nearly dying, etcetera?' gasped Johnny.

'Yup.'

'Me too. I've been shooting some really disreputable speed, made by a failed chemistry graduate with a shaking hand and a bottle of hydrochloric acid. It's the kind that smells of burnt test-tubes when you push the plunger down, and then makes you sneeze compulsively, sending your heart into wild arhythmic flurries reminiscent of the worst passages of Pound's *Cantos*.'

'As long as your Chinese is good you should be all right.'

'I haven't got any.'

'I have. It's medicine, man, medicine.'

'I'm coming over.'

'To New York?'

113

'New York! I thought the hesitating, whispering quality of your speech was a combination of my auditory hallucinations and your notorious indolence. It's very disappointing to learn that it has a *real* cause. Why are you there?'

'My father died over here, so I've come to collect his remains.'

'Congratulations. You've achieved half-orphan status like me. Are they refusing to part with his body? Are they making you put an equal weight of gold in the opposite scales to secure the precious cargo?'

'They haven't billed me for it yet, but if there's even a hint of exaggeration, I'll just leave the rotten thing behind.'

'Good thinking. Are you at all upset?'

'I feel rather haunted.'

'Yes. I remember finding that the ground beneath my feet seemed, if possible, more unreliable than usual, and that my desire to die was, if possible, even greater than before.'

'Yes, there's a lot of that. Plus quite a bad pain in my liver, as if a grave-digger had dug a shovel under my ribs and stepped on it rather hard.'

'That's what your liver's for, didn't you know?'

'How can you ask that?'

'It's true. Forgive me. So when are we two Olympians going to meet?'

'Well, I should be back tomorrow evening. Could you get some gear, and then I'll come straight round to you from the airport, without having to see the appalling Brian.'

'Of course. Talking of appalling people, I wound up in the flat of some truly idiotic Italians the other night, but they did have some pink crystal coke which made a sound like a glockenspiel when it dropped into the spoon. Anyhow, I stole the whole lot and locked myself in the bathroom. As you know it takes a lot to ruffle the moronic tranquillity of those doe-eyed Italian dope-fiends, but they seemed *really* pissed off, banging on the door and shouting, "Come out of there, you fucking man, or I kill you. Alessandro, make him come out!" '

'God, how hilarious.'

'Sadly, I think we've said "Ciao" for the last time, or I'd get you some. It was really the stuff to take before pushing the flaming longship into the grey waters for the last time.'

'You're making me envious.'

'Well, maybe we'll finally kill ourselves tomorrow night.'

'Definitely. Make sure you get a lot.'

'Yup.'

'Okay, I'll see you tomorrow evening.'

'Goodbye.'

'Bye now.'

Patrick hung up the phone with a faint smile on his lips. It always cheered one up talking to Johnny.

He immediately dialled a new set of numbers and settled back on the pillows.

'Hello?'

'Kay?'

'Baby! How are you? Hang on, I'll just turn down the music.'

The sound of an exasperated solitary cello grew suddenly muted, and Kay returned to the phone. 'So how are you?' she asked again.

'I haven't managed to get very much sleep.'

'I'm not surprised.'

'Neither am I, I've had about four grams of coke.'

'Oh, God, that's awful. You haven't been taking heroin as well, have you?'

'No, no, no. I've given that up. Just a few tranquillisers.'

'Well, that's something, but why the coke? Think of your poor nose. You can't let it just drop off.'

'My nose is going to be fine. I just felt so depressed.'

'Poor baby, I'm sure you did. Your father dying is the worst thing that could have happened to you. You never got a chance to work things out.'

'We never would have.'

'That's what all sons feel.'

'Mm . . .'

'I don't like to think of you there alone. Are you seeing anybody nice today, or just morticians?'

'Are you implying that morticians can't be nice?' asked Patrick lugubriously.

'Lord, no, I think they do a wonderful job.'

'I don't really know. I have to collect the ashes,

116

otherwise I'm as free as the wind. I wish you were here.'

'So do I, but I'll see you tomorrow, won't I?'

'Absolutely. I'll come round straight from the airport.' Patrick lit a cigarette. 'I've been thinking all night,' he continued rapidly, ' – if you can call that thinking – about whether ideas come from the continual need to talk, relieved occasionally by the paralysing presence of other people, or if we simply realise in speech what we've already thought.' He hoped this was the kind of question that would distract Kay from the exact details of his return.

'That shouldn't have kept you up,' she laughed. 'I'll tell you the answer tomorrow night. What time do you get in?'

'Around ten,' said Patrick, adding a few hours to the arrival time.

'So I'll see you about eleven?'

'Perfect.'

'Bye, baby. Lots of love.'

'You too. Bye now.'

Patrick put down the phone and made himself another little fix of coke to keep him going. The last fix was still too recent and he had to lie on the bed for a while, sweating, before he could make the next call.

'Hello? Debbie?'

'Darling. I didn't dare call you in case you were asleep.'

'That hasn't been my problem.'

'Well, I'm sorry, I didn't know that.'

'I'm not accusing you of anything. There's no need to be so defensive.'

'I'm not being defensive,' laughed Debbie. 'I was just worried about you. This is ridiculous. I only meant that I've been worried all night about how you were.'

'Ridiculous, I suppose.'

'Oh, please don't let's argue. I wasn't saying *you* were ridiculous. I meant that arguing is ridiculous.'

'Well, I was arguing, and if arguing is ridiculous then I was being ridiculous. My case rests.'

'What case? You always think I'm attacking you. We're not in a courtroom, I'm not your opponent or your enemy.'

Silence. Patrick's head pounded from the effort of not contradicting her. 'So what did you do last night?' he asked at last.

'Well, I was trying to get hold of you for a long time, and then I went to Gregory and Rebecca's dinner thing.'

'Suffering takes place while somebody else is eating. Who said that?'

'It could have been almost anyone,' laughed Debbie.

'It just popped into my mind.'

'Mm. You should try editing some of the things that just pop into your mind.'

'Well, never mind last night, what are you doing tomorrow night?'

'We've been asked to China's thing, but I don't suppose you want to eat and suffer at the same time.' Debbie laughed at her own joke, as was her habit, while Patrick pursued his ruthless policy of never laughing at anything she said, without feeling on this occasion the least trace of meanness.

'What a brilliant remark,' he said drily. 'I won't come along, but nothing could persuade me to stop you from going.'

'Don't be ridiculous, I'll cancel.'

'It sounds as if I had better not stop being ridiculous, or you won't recognise me. I was going to come and see you straight from the airport, but I'll come when you get back from China's. At twelve or one.'

'Well, okay, but I'll cancel if you like.'

'No, no, I wouldn't dream of it.'

'I'd better not go or you'll just use it against me later.'

'We're not in a courtroom. I'm not your opponent or your enemy,' Patrick echoed mockingly.

Silence. Debbie waited until she could make a fresh start, trying to ignore Patrick's impossibly contradictory demands.

'Are you in the Pierre?' she asked brightly.

'If you don't know what hotel I'm in, how could you have rung me?'

'I guessed you were in the Pierre, but I couldn't be sure since you didn't see fit to tell me,' sighed Debbie. 'Is the room lovely?'

'I think you would like it. There are lots of sachets in the bathroom and a phone next to the loo, so you needn't miss any important calls – an invitation to dinner at China's, for instance.'

'Why are you being so horrid?'

'Am I?'

'I'm going to cancel tomorrow.'

'No, no, *please* don't. It was only a joke. I feel rather mad at the moment.'

'You always feel rather mad,' laughed Debbie.

'Well, my father happens to have died, which makes me feel especially mad.'

'I know, darling, I'm sorry.'

'Plus, I've taken a huge quantity of coke.'

'Was that a good idea?'

'Of course it wasn't a good idea,' yelped Patrick indignantly.

'Do you think your father's death will make you less like him?' Debbie sighed again.

'I'll have the work of two to do now.'

'God, are you sure you wouldn't rather forget the whole thing?'

'Of course I'd rather forget the whole thing,' snapped Patrick, 'but that's not an option.'

'Well, everyone has their cross to bear.'

'Really? What's yours?'

'You,' laughed Debbie.

'Well, be careful or somebody might steal it from you.'

'They'll have to fight for it,' said Debbie affection-
ately.

'Sweet,' cooed Patrick, wedging the phone between
his shoulder and his ear and sitting on the edge of
the bed.

'Oh, darling, why do we always argue?' asked
Debbie.

'Because we're so in love,' said Patrick haphaz-
ardly, as he opened the packet of heroin over the
bedside table. He dipped his little finger in the
powder, put it to one of his nostrils and inhaled
quietly.

'That would seem a strange explanation from anybody else.'

'Well, I hope you're not getting it from anybody
else,' said Patrick babyishly, dipping and sniffing
several more times.

'Nobody else would dare give it, if they behaved
like you,' laughed Debbie.

'It's just that I need you so much,' whispered
Patrick, reclining again on the pillows. 'It's frighten-
ing if you're addicted to independence like I am.'

'Oh, that's what you're addicted to, is it?'

'Yes. All the other things are illusions.'

'Am I an illusion?'

'No! That's why we argue so much. Do you see?'
It sounded good to him.

'Because I'm a *real* obstacle to your independence?'

'To my foolish and misguided desire for independence,' Patrick corrected her gallantly.

'Well, you certainly know how to pay a girl a compliment,' laughed Debbie.

'I wish you were here,' croaked Patrick, dabbing his finger in the white powder again.

'So do I, you must be having a horrible time. Why don't you go and see Marianne? – she'll look after you.'

'What a good idea. I'll give her a ring later on.'

'I'd better go now,' sighed Debbie. 'I've got to be interviewed by some silly magazine.'

'What for?'

'Oh, about people who go to lots of parties. I don't know why I agreed to it.'

'Because you're so kind and helpful,' said Patrick.

'Mm . . . I'll call you later. I think you're being very brave and I love you.'

'I love you too.'

'Bye, darling.'

'Bye now.'

Patrick hung up the phone and glanced at the clock. Six-thirty-five. He ordered Canadian bacon, fried eggs, toast, porridge, stewed fruit, orange juice, coffee, and tea.

'Is that breakfast for two?' asked the cheerful-sounding woman taking the order.

'No, just for one.'

'Wooh, you're sure having a hearty breakfast, honey,' she giggled.

'It's the best way to start the day, don't you find?'

'Sure is!' she agreed.

CHAPTER NINE

The smell of decaying food had filled the room surprisingly quickly. Patrick's breakfast was devastated without being eaten. A dent in the grey paste of the porridge contained a half-eaten stewed pear; rashers of bacon hung on the edge of a plate smeared with egg yolk, and in the flooded saucer two cigarette butts lay sodden with coffee. A triangle of abandoned toast bore the semi-circular imprint of his teeth, and spilt sugar glistened everywhere on the table-cloth. Only the orange juice and the tea were completely finished.

On the television, the wily coyote, astride an accelerating rocket, crashed explosively into the side of a mountain, while the Road Runner disappeared into a tunnel, emerged the other side, and receded in a cloud of dust. Watching the Road Runner and the stylised rotundity of the dust in his wake, Patrick was reminded of the early, innocent days of his drug-taking, when he had thought that LSD would reveal to him something other than the tyranny of its own effects on his consciousness.

123

Thanks to his loathing of air-conditioning the room was becoming increasingly muggy. Patrick longed to wheel the trolley outside, but the danger of meeting someone in the corridor made him resigned to the growing stench. He had already over-heard a conversation about himself between two maids, and although he accepted, theoretically, that it was a hallucination, his strength of mind would not allow him to test this vein of detachment to the extent of opening the door. After all, had one maid not said to the other, 'I told him, "You gonna die, boy, if you go on takin' that shit." ' And hadn't the other one replied, 'You gotta call the police for your own protection, can't go on livin' like that.'

Wandering into the bathroom, he rolled his right shoulder to ease the pain that was lodged under the shoulderblade. Sceptically but irresistibly, he approached the mirror and noticed that one of his eyelids was drooping much lower than the other, drooping over an inflamed and watering eye. Pulling the skin down he saw the familiar dark yellow of his eyeballs. His tongue was also yellow and thickly coated. Only the purple trenches under his eyes relieved the deadly whiteness of his complexion.

Thank God his father had died. Without a dead parent there was really no excuse for looking so awful. He thought of one of the guiding mottoes of his father's life: 'Never apologise, never explain.'

'What the fuck else is there to do?' muttered Patrick, turning on the taps of his bath and tearing open one of the sachets with his teeth. As he poured the glutinous green liquid into the swirling water he heard, or thought he heard, the ringing of the telephone. Was it the management warning him that the police were on their way up? Whoever it was, the outside world was crashing into his atmosphere, and it filled him with dread. He turned off the taps and listened to the naked ringing of the phone. Why answer? And yet he couldn't bear not to; maybe he was going to be saved.

Sitting on the loo seat, not trusting his own voice, Patrick picked up the phone and said, 'Hello?'

'Patrick, my dear,' drawled a voice from the other end.

'George!'

'Is this a bad time to call?'

'Not at all.'

'I was wondering if you'd like to have lunch with me. It may be the last thing you want to do, of course. You must be feeling perfectly ghastly. It's a terrible shock, you know, Patrick, we all feel that.'

'I do feel a bit wonky, but I'd love to have lunch.'

'I must warn you, I've asked some other people. Charming people, naturally, the nicest sort of Americans. One or two of them have met your father and liked him very much.'

'It sounds perfect,' said Patrick, raising his eyes to the ceiling and grimacing.

'I'm meeting them at the Key Club. Do you know it?'

'No.'

'I think you'll find it amusing in its way. One comes in from the noise and the pollution of New York, and it's quite suddenly like an English country house of a certain sort. God knows whose family they are – I suppose some of the members must have lent them – but the walls are covered in portraits, and the effect is really quite charming. There are all the usual things one would expect to find, like Gentleman's Relish for instance, and strangely enough some things that are nowadays very hard to find in England, like a good Bullshot. Your father and I agreed that we hadn't had such a good Bullshot in years.'

'It sounds heaven.'

'I've asked Ballantine Morgan. I don't know if you've met him. I'm afraid I'm not sure he isn't the most frightful bore, but Sarah has taken to him in a big way and one gets so used to his popping up everywhere that I've asked him to lunch. Oddly enough, I knew someone called Morgan Ballantine once, perfectly charming man; they must be related in some way, but I've never really got to the bottom of it,' said George wistfully.

'Perhaps we'll find out today,' said Patrick.

'Well, I'm not sure I can ask Ballantine again. I have a feeling I must have asked him before, but it's very hard to be sure because one has such trouble listening to his answers.'

'What time shall we meet?'

'About quarter to one in the bar.'

'Perfect.'

'Well, goodbye, my dear.'

'Bye now. See you at quarter to one.' Patrick's voice trailed off.

He turned his bath back on and wandered into the bedroom to pour himself a glass of bourbon. A bath without a drink was like – was like a bath without a drink. Was there any need to elaborate or compare?

A voice on the television spoke excitedly about a complete set of prestigious carving knives, accompanied by an incredible wok, a beautiful set of salad bowls, a book of mouthwatering recipes and, as if this wasn't enough, a machine for cutting vegetables into different shapes. Patrick glazed over as he stared at carrots being sliced, diced, shredded and cubed.

The mound of shaved ice in which his orange juice had arrived turned out to be completely melted and Patrick, suddenly frustrated, kicked the breakfast trolley and sent it thudding into the wall. He was overwhelmed with despair at the prospect of having no ice in his drink. What was the point of going on? Everything was wrong, everything was hopelessly fucked up. He sat down, defenceless and defeated, on the edge of the bed, the bottle of bourbon held loosely in one hand. He had imagined an icy glass of bourbon resting steamily on the side of the bath, had wagered all his hope on it, but finding that the plan was compromised, nothing stood between him and utter bankruptcy. He drank a gulp straight from the bottle and put it down on the bedside table. It stung his throat and made him shudder.

The clock showed eleven-twenty. He must get into action and prepare himself for the business of the day. Now was the time for speed and alcohol. He must leave the coke behind, or he would spend the whole of lunch shooting up in the loo, as usual.

He got up from the bed and suddenly punched the lampshade, sending the lamp crashing to the carpet. With the bottle of bourbon in his hand, he walked back into the bathroom, where he found the water gently overflowing from the side of the bath and flooding the floor. Refusing to panic or show any surprise, he slowly turned off the water and pushed the sodden bathmat around with his foot, spreading the water into the corners it had not yet reached. He undressed, getting his trousers wet, and tossed his clothes through the open door.

The bath was absurdly hot and Patrick had to pull the plug out and run the cold water before he could climb in. Once he was lying in it, it seemed too cold again. He reached for the bottle of bourbon he had put on the floor beside the bath, and for no reason that he could make out he poured the bourbon from the air and sucked it in as it splashed and trickled over his face.

The bottle was soon empty and he held it under the water, watching the bubbles run out of the neck and then moving it around the bottom of the bath like a submarine stalking enemy ships.

Looking down, he caught sight of his arms and drew in his breath sharply and involuntarily. Among the fading yellow bruises, and the pink threads of old scars, a fresh set of purple wounds clustered around his main veins and at odd points along his arm. At the centre of this unhealthy canvas was the black bulge produced by the missed shot of the night before. The thought that this was his own arm ambushed Patrick quite suddenly, and made him want to cry. He closed his eyes and sank under the surface of the water, breathing out violently from his nose. It didn't bear thinking about.

As he surged out of the water, flicking his head from side to side, Patrick was surprised to hear the phone ring again.

He got out of the bath, and picked up the phone beside the loo. These bathroom phones were really quite useful – perhaps it was China asking him to dinner, begging him to reconsider.

'Yes?' he drawled.

'Hey, Patrick?' said an unmistakable voice on the other end.

'Marianne! How sweet of you to ring.'

'I'm so *sorry* to hear about your father,' said Marianne in a voice that was hesitating but deeply self-assured, whispering but husky. It seemed not to be projected from her body into the world, but to draw the world inside her body; she did not speak so much as swallow articulately. Anyone who listened to her was forced to imagine her long smooth throat, and the elegant S of her body, exaggerated by the extraordinary curve of her spine that made her breasts swell further forward and her bottom further back.

Why had he never been to bed with her? The fact that she had never shown any signs of desire for him had played an unhelpful role, but that might be attributed to her friendship with Debbie. How could she resist him after all? thought Patrick, glancing in the mirror.

Fucking hell. He was going to have to rely on her pity.

'Well, you know how it is,' he drawled sarcastically. 'Death, where is thy sting?'

'Of all the evils in the world which are reproached with an evil character, death is the most innocent of its accusation.'

'Bang on in this case,' said Patrick. 'Who said that anyhow?'

'Bishop Taylor in *The Correct Rules for Holy Dying*,' Marianne disclosed.

'Your favourite book?'

'It's *so* great,' she gasped hoarsely; 'I swear to God, it's the most beautiful prose I've ever read.'

She was clever too. It was really intolerable; he had to have her.

'Will you have dinner with me?' Patrick asked.

'Oh, God, I wish . . .' gasped Marianne, 'but I've got to have dinner with my parents. Do you want to come along?'

'That would be wonderful,' said Patrick, annoyed not to have her to himself.

'Good. I'll let my parents know,' she purred. 'Come on over to their apartment around seven o'clock.'

'Perfect,' said Patrick, and then, unguardedly, 'I adore you.'

'Hey!' said Marianne ambiguously. 'See you later.'

Patrick hung up the phone. He had to have her, he definitely had to have her. She was not merely the latest object on which his greedy desire to be saved had fixed itself; no, she was the woman who was going to save him. The woman whose fine intelligence and deep sympathy and divine body, yes, whose divine body would successfully deflect his attention from the gloomy well-shaft of his feelings and the contemplation of his past.

If he got her he would give up drugs for ever, or at least have someone really attractive to take them with. He giggled wildly, wrapping a towel around himself and striding back into his bedroom with renewed vigour.

He looked like shit, it was true, but everybody knew that what women really valued, apart from a great deal of money, was gentleness and humour. Gentleness was not his speciality, and he wasn't feeling especially funny, but this was a case of destiny: he had to have her or he would die.

It was time to get practical, to take a Black Beauty and lock the coke in his suitcase. He fished a capsule out of his jacket and swallowed it with impressive efficiency. As he tidied away the coke he could see no reason not to have one last fix. After all, he hadn't had one for almost forty minutes and he would not be having another for a couple of hours. Too lazy to go through the entire ritual, he stuck the needle into an easily accessible vein in the back of his hand and administered the injection.

The effects were certainly growing weaker, he noted, still able to walk around, if a little shakily, with his shoulders hunched high up beside his ears, and his jaw tightly clenched.

It was really unbearable to contemplate being separated from the coke for so long, but he couldn't control himself if he carried supplies with him. The sensible thing to do was to prepare a couple of fixes, one in the rather tired old syringe he had been using all night, its rubber plunger now tending to stick to the sides of the barrel, and the other in the precious untouched syringe. Just as some men wore a handkerchief in their breast pockets to cope with the emergency of a woman's tears, or a sneeze, he often tucked away a couple of syringes into the same pocket to cope with the endlessly renewed emptiness that invaded him. Pip! Pip! Be prepared!

Suffering from yet another aural hallucination, Patrick overheard a conversation between a policeman and a member of the hotel staff.

'Was this guy a regular?'

'Na, he was the-holiday-of-a-lifetime type.'

'Ya, ya,' muttered Patrick impatiently. He wasn't that easily intimidated.

He put on a clean white shirt, slipped into his second suit, a dark grey herring-bone, stepping into his shoes at the same time as he did up his gold cufflinks. His silver and black tie, unfortunately the only one he had, was flecked with blood, but he managed, by tying it rather too short, to disguise the fact, although he had to tuck the longer strip into his shirt, a practice he despised.

Less easily solved was the problem of his left eye, which had now completely closed, except for an occasional nervous fluttering. He could, with great effort, open it up but only by raising his eyebrows to a position of high indignation. On his way to the Key Club, he would have to go to the pharmacy and get himself an eyepatch.

His breast pocket was deep enough to conceal the raised plungers of the two syringes, and the bag of smack fitted neatly into the ticket pocket of his jacket. Everything was completely under control, except that he was sweating like a stuck pig and couldn't shake off the sense that he had forgotten something crucial.

Patrick took the chain off the door and glanced back nostalgically at the fetid dark chaos he was leaving behind. The curtains were still closed, the bed unmade, pillows and clothes on the floor, the lamp overturned, the trolley of food rotting in the warm atmosphere, the bathroom flooded and the television, where a man was shouting, 'Come to Crazy Eddie's! The prices are *insane*,' still flickering.

Stepping out into the corridor, Patrick could not help noticing a policeman standing outside the next-door room.

His overcoat! That was what he had forgotten. But if he doubled back wouldn't it look guilty?

He hovered in the doorway, and then muttered loudly, 'Oh yes, I must . . .', drawing the police-man's attention to himself as he strode back appalled into his room. What were the police doing there? Could they tell what he'd been doing?

His overcoat felt heavy and less reassuring than usual. He mustn't take too long or they would wonder what he was up to.

'You're gonna fry in that coat,' said the policeman with a smile.

'It's not a crime, is it?' asked Patrick, more aggres-sively than he'd intended.

'Normally,' said the policeman with mock serious-ness, 'we'd have to arrest ya, but we got our hands full,' he added with a resigned shrug.

'What happened here?' asked Patrick in his MP-with-the-constituent manner.

'Guy died of a heart attack.'

'The party's over,' said Patrick with a private sense of pleasure.

'There was a party here last night?' the policeman was suddenly curious.

'NO, no, I just meant . . .' Patrick felt he was coming from too many directions at once.

'You heard no noises, cries, nothing unusual?'

'No, I heard nothing.'

The policeman relaxed, and ran his hand over his largely bald scalp. 'You're from England, right?'

'That's right.'

'I could tell from the accent.'

'They'll make you a detective soon,' said Patrick boisterously. He waved as he set off down the long carpet of gushing pink and green flower-laden urns, with the policeman's imagined eyebeams burning into his back.

CHAPTER TEN

Patrick sprang up the steps of the Key Club with unaccustomed eagerness, his nerves squirming like a bed of maggots whose protective stone has been flicked aside, exposing them to the assault of the open sky. Wearing an eyepatch, he hurried gratefully into the gloomy hall of the club, his shirt clinging to his sweating back.

The hall porter took his overcoat in silent surprise and led him down a narrow corridor, its walls covered with memorials to remarkable dogs, horses and servants, and one or two cartoons bearing witness to the feeble and long-forgotten eccentricities of certain dead members. It really was a temple of English virtues as George had promised.

Ushered into a large pannelled room full of green and brown leather armchairs of Victorian design, and huge glossy paintings of dogs holding birds in their obedient mouths, Patrick saw George in the corner, already in conversation with another man.

'Patrick, my dear, how are you?'

'Hello, George.'

'Is there something wrong with your eye?'

'Just a little inflammation.'

'Oh, dear, well, I hope it clears up,' said George sincerely. 'Do you know Ballantine Morgan?' he asked, turning to a small man with weak blue eyes, neat white hair, and a well-trimmed moustache.

'Hello Patrick,' said Ballantine, giving him a firm handshake. Patrick noticed that he was wearing a black silk tie and wondered if he was in mourning for some reason.

'I was very sorry to hear about your father,' said Ballantine. 'I didn't know him personally, but from everything George tells me it sounds like he was a great English gentleman.'

Jesus Christ, thought Patrick.

'What have you been telling him?' he asked George reproachfully.

'Only what an exceptional man your father was.'

'Yes, I'm pleased to say that he was exceptional,' said Patrick. 'I've never met anybody quite like him.'

'He refused to compromise,' drawled George. 'What was it he used to say? "Nothing but the best, or go without." '

'Always felt the same way myself,' said Ballantine fatuously.

'Would you like a drink?' asked George.

'I'll have one of those Bullshots you spoke about so passionately this morning.'

'Passionately,' guffawed Ballantine.

'Well, there are some things one feels passionately about,' smiled George, looking at the barman and

138

briefly raising his index finger. 'I shall feel quite bereft without your father,' he continued. 'Oddly enough, it was here that we were supposed to be having lunch on the day that he died. The last time I met him we went to a perfectly extraordinary place that has an arrangement of some sort – I can't believe that it's reciprocal – with the Travellers' in Paris. The protraits were at least four times life size – we laughed about that a good deal – he was on very good form, although, of course, there was always an undercurrent of disappointment with your father. I think he really enjoyed himself on this last visit. You must never forget, Patrick, that he was very proud of you. I'm sure you know that. Really proud.'

Patrick felt sick.

Ballantine looked bored, as people do when someone they don't know is being discussed. He had a very natural desire to talk about himself, but felt that a little pause was in order.

'Yes,' said George to the waiter, 'we'd like two Bullshots and . . .' He leant inquiringly towards Ballantine.

'I'll have another Martini,' said Ballantine.

There was a short silence.

'What a lot of faithful gundogs,' said Patrick wearily, glancing around the room.

'I suppose a lot of the members are keen shots,' said George. 'Ballantine is one of the best shots in the world.'

'Whoa, whoa, whoa,' protested Ballantine, '*used* to

139

be the best shot in the world.' He held out his hand to arrest the flow of self-congratulation, but was no more effective than King Canute in the face of another great force of nature. 'What I haven't lost,' he couldn't help pointing out, 'is a gun collection which is probably the greatest in the world.'

The waiter returned with the drinks.

'Would you bring me the book called *The Morgan Gun Collection*?' Ballantine asked him.

'Yes, Mr Morgan,' said the waiter in a voice that suggested he had dealt with this request before.

Patrick tasted the Bullshot and found himself smiling irresistibly. He drank half of it in one gulp, put it down for a moment, picked it up again and said to George, 'You were right about these Bullshots,' drinking the rest.

'Would you like another one?' asked George.

'I think I will, they're so delicious.'

The waiter weaved his way back to the table with an enormous white volume. On the front cover, visible from some way off, was a photograph of two silver-inlaid pistols.

'Here you are, Mr Morgan,' said the waiter.

'Ahh-aa,' said Ballantine, taking the book.

'And another Bullshot, would you?' said George.

'Yes, sir.'

Ballantine tried to suppress a grin of pride. 'These guns right here,' he said, tapping the front cover of the book, 'are a pair of Spanish seventeenth-century duelling pistols which are the most valuable firearms in the world. If I tell you that the triggers cost over a million dollars to replace, you'll have some idea of what I mean.'

'It's enough to make you wonder if it's worth fighting a duel,' said Patrick.

'The original cleaning brushes alone are worth over a quarter of a million dollars,' chuckled Ballantine, 'so you wouldn't want to fire the pistols too often.'

George looked pained and distant, but Ballantine in his role as The Triumph of Life, performing the valuable task of distracting Patrick from his terrible grief, was unstoppable. He put on a pair of tortoise-shell half-moon spectacles, pushed his head back and looked condescendingly at his book, while he allowed the pages to flicker past.

'This here,' he said, stopping the flow of pages and holding the book open towards Patrick, 'this is the first Winchester Repeating Rifle ever manufactured.'

'Amazing,' sighed Patrick.

'When I was shooting in Africa, I brought down a lion with this gun,' admitted Ballantine. 'It took a number of shots – it doesn't have the calibre of a modern weapon.'

'You must have been all the more grateful for the repeating mechanism,' Patrick suggested.

'Oh, I was covered by a couple of reliable hunters,' said Ballantine complacently. 'I describe the incident in the book I wrote about my African hunting trips.'

The waiter returned with Patrick's second Bullshot, and another large book under his arm.

'Harry thought you might want this as well, Mr Morgan.'

'Well, I'll be darned,' said Ballantine with a colloquial twang, craning back in his chair and beaming at the barman. 'I mentioned the book and it falls in my lap. Now that's what I call service!'

He opened the new volume with familiar relish. 'Some of my friends have been kind enough to say that I have an excellent prose style,' he explained in a voice that did not sound as puzzled as it was meant to. 'I don't see it myself, I just put it down as it was. The way I hunted in Africa is a way of life that doesn't exist any more, and I just told the truth about it, that's all.'

'Yes,' drawled George. 'Journalists and people of that sort write a lot of nonsense about what they call the "Happy Valley Set". Well, I was there a good deal at the time, and I can tell you there was no more unhappiness than usual, no more drunkenness than usual, people behaved just as they did in London or New York.'

George leant over and picked up an olive. 'We did have dinner in our pyjamas,' he added thoughtfully, 'which I suppose *was* a little unusual. But not because we all wanted to jump into bed with one another, although obviously a good deal of that sort of thing went on, as it always does; it was simply that we had to get up the next day at dawn to go hunting. When we got back in the afternoon, we would have "Toasty", which would be a whisky and soda, or whatever you wanted. And then they would say, "Bathy, bwana, bathy time," and run you a bath. After that more "Toasty", and then dinner in one's pyjamas. People behaved just as they did anywhere else, although I must say, they did drink a great deal, really a great deal.'

'It sounds like heaven,' said Patrick.

'Well, you know, George, the drinking went with the lifestyle. You just sweated it all out,' said Ballantine.

'Yes, quite,' said George.

You don't have to go to Africa to sweat too much, thought Patrick.

'This is a photograph of me with a Tanganyikan Mountain Goat,' said Ballantine, handing Patrick the second book. 'I was told that it was the last potent male of the species, so I can't help having mixed feelings about it.'

God, he's sensitive too, thought Patrick, looking at the photograph of a younger Ballantine, in a khaki hat, kneeling beside the corpse of a goat.

'I took the photographs myself,' said Ballantine casually. 'A number of professional photographers have begged me to tell them my "secret", but I've had to disappoint them – the only secret is to get a fascinating subject and photograph it the best way you know how.'

'Amazing,' mumbled Patrick.

'Sometimes, from a foolish impulse of pride,' Ballantine continued, 'I included myself in the shots and allowed one of the boys to press the trigger – they could do that well enough.'

'Ah,' said George with uncharacteristic verve, 'here's Tom.'

An exceptionally tall man in a blue seersucker suit worked his way through the tables. He had thin but rather chaotic grey hair, and drooping bloodhound eyes.

Ballantine closed the two books and rested them on his knees. The loop of his monstrous vanity was complete. He had been talking about a book in which he wrote about his photographs of the animals he had shot with guns from his own magnificent collection, a collection photographed (alas, not by him) in the second book.

'Tom Charles,' said George, 'Patrick Melrose.'

'I see you've been talking to the Renaissance Man,' said Tom in a dry gravelly voice. 'How are you, Ballantine? Been keeping Mr Melrose up to date on your achievements?'

'Well, I thought he might be interested in the guns,' said Ballantine peevishly.

'The thought he never has, is that somebody might *not* be interested in the guns,' Tom croaked. 'I was sorry to hear about your father, I guess you must be feeling sick at heart.'

'I suppose I am,' said Patrick, caught off balance.

'It's a terrible time for anybody. Whatever you feel, you feel it strongly, and you feel just about everything.'

'Do you want a drink, or do you want to go straight in to lunch?' asked George.

'Let's eat,' said Tom.

The four men got up. Patrick noticed that the two Bullshots had made him feel much more substantial. He could also detect the steady lucid throb of the speed. Perhaps he could allow himself a quick fix before lunch.

'Where are the loos, George?'

'Oh, just through that door in the corner,' said George. 'We'll be in the dining room, up the stairs on the right.'

'I'll see you there.'

Patrick broke away from the group and headed for the door that George had pointed out. On the other side he found a large cool room of black and white marble, shiny chrome fittings and mahogany doors. At one end of a row of basins was a pile of starched linen with 'Key Club' sewn into the corner in green cotton, and, beside it, a large wicker basket for discarding the used towels.

With sudden efficiency and stealth, he picked up a towel, filled a glass with water, and slipped into one of the mahogany cubicles.

There was no time to waste and Patrick seemed to put the glass down, drop the towel and take off his jacket in one gesture.

He sat on the loo seat and put the syringe carefully on the towel in his lap. He rolled his sleeve up tightly on his bicep to act as a makeshift tourniquet and, while he frantically clenched and unclenched his fist, removed the cap of the syringe with the thumb of his other hand.

His veins were becoming quite shy, but a lucky stab in the bicep, just below his rolled-up sleeve, yielded the gratifying spectacle of a red mushroom cloud uncurling in the barrel of the syringe.

He pushed the plunger down hard and unrolled his shirt as fast as he could to allow the solution a free passage through his bloodstream.

Patrick wiped the trickle of blood from his arm and flushed out the syringe, also squirting its pinkish water into the towel.

The rush was disappointing. Although his hands were shaking and his heart was pounding, he had missed that blissful fainting sensation, that heartbreaking moment, as compressed as the autobiography of a drowning man, but as elusive and intimate as the smell of a flower.

What was the fucking point of shooting coke if he wasn't going to get a proper rush? It was intolerable.

Indignant and yet anxious about the consequences, Patrick took out the second syringe, sat down on the loo again and rolled up his sleeve. The strange thing was that the rush seemed to be getting stronger, as if it had been dammed up against his shirt sleeve and had taken unusually long to reach his brain. In any case he was now committed to a second fix and, with a combination of bowel-loosening excitement and dread, he tried to put the spike back in exactly the same spot as before.

As he rolled down his sleeve this time, he realised that he had made a serious mistake. This was too much. Only far too much was enough. But this was more than enough.

Too overwhelmed to flush it out, he only managed to put the cap back on the precious new syringe and drop it on the floor. He slumped against the back wall of the cubicle, his head hanging to one side, gasping and wincing like an athlete who has just crossed the finishing line after losing a race, the prickle of fresh sweat breaking out all over the surface of his skin, and his eyes tightly closed while a rapid succession of scenes flashed across his inner vision: a bee crashing drunkenly into the pollen-laden pistils of a flower; fissures spreading over the concrete of a disintegrating dam; a long blade cutting strips of flesh from the body of a dead whale; a barrel of gouged-out eyes tumbling stickily between the cylinders of a wine-press.

He forced his eyes open. His inner life was definitely *in decline* and it would be more cautious to go upstairs and face the confusing effects of other people than sink any further into this pool of discreet and violent imagery.

The aural hallucinations that afflicted Patrick as he groped his way along the wall towards the line of basins were not yet organised into words, but consisted of twisting strands of sound and an eerie sense of space, like amplified breathing.

He mopped his face and emptied the glass of bloody water down the drain. Remembering the second syringe, he quickly tried to clean it out, watching the reflection of the door in the mirror in case somebody came in. His hands shook so badly it was hard to hold the needle under the tap.

It must have been ages since he left the others. They were probably ordering the bill by now. Short of breath, but with insane urgency, he stuffed the wet syringe back into his breast pocket and hurried back through the bar, into the hall, and up the main staircase.

In the dining room he saw George, Tom and Ballantine still reading the menu. How long had he kept them waiting, politely postponing their lunch? He moved clumsily towards the table, the strands of curving, twisting sound bending the space around him.

George looked up.

'Ziouuu . . . Ziouuu . . . Ziouuu . . .' he asked.

'Chok-chok-chok-chok,' said Ballantine, like a helicopter.

'Aioua. Aioua,' Tom suggested.

What the fuck were they trying to tell him? Patrick sat down and mopped his face with the pale pink napkin.

'Sot,' he said in a long elastic whisper.

'Chok-chok-chok,' Ballantine replied.

George was smiling, but Patrick listened helplessly as the sounds streamed past him like a photograph of brake lights on a wet street.

'Ziou . . . Ziou . . . Ziou . . . Aiou. Aiou. Chok-chok-chok.'

He sat astonished in front of the menu, as if he had never seen one before. There were pages of dead things – cows, shrimps, pigs, oysters, lambs – stretched out like a casualty list, accompanied by a brief description of how they had been treated since they died – skewered, grilled, smoked and boiled. Christ, if they thought he was going to eat these things they must be mad.

He had seen the dark blood from the neck of a sheep gushing into the dry grass. The busy flies. The stench of offal. He had heard the roots tearing as he eased a carrot out of the ground. Any living man squatted on a mound of corruption, cruelty, filth and blood.

If only his body would turn into a pane of glass, the fleshless interval between two spaces, knowing both but belonging to neither, then he would be set free from the gross and savage debt he owed to the rest of nature.

'Ziou . . . Ziou . . . wan?' asked George.

'Um . . . I'll . . . um, eh just.' Patrick felt remote from his own voice, as if it was coming out of his feet. 'I'll . . . um, eh, have . . . another . . . Bullshot . . . late breakfast . . . eh . . . not really hungry.'

The effort of saying these few words left him breathless.

'Chok-chok-chok-chok,' objected Ballantine.

'Aioua sure. Aioua ziou?' asked Tom.

What was he saying 'Ziou' for? The fugue was growing more complicated. Before long George would be saying 'Chok' or 'Aioua', and then where would he stand? Where would any of them stand?

'Justanothershot,' gasped Patrick, 'really.'

Mopping his brow again, he stared fixedly at the stem of his wineglass which, caught by the sun, cast a fractured bone of light onto the white table-cloth, like an X-ray of a broken finger. The twisting echoing sounds around him had started to die down to the faint hiss of an untuned television. It was no longer incomprehension but a kind of sadness, like an enormously amplified post-coital gloom, that cut him off from what was happening around him.

'Martha Boeing,' Ballantine was saying, 'told me that she was experiencing dizzy spells on the drive up to Newport and that her doctor told her to take along these small French cheeses to eat on the journey – evidently it was some kind of protein deprivation.'

'I can't imagine that Martha's malnutrition is too severe,' said Tom.

'Well,' remarked George diplomatically, 'not everybody has to be driven to Newport as often as she does.'

'I mention it because I,' said Ballantine with some pride, 'was getting the same symptoms.'

'On the same journey?' asked Tom.

'The exact same journey,' Ballantine confirmed.

'Well, that's Newport for you,' said Tom; 'sucks the protein right out of you. Only sporting types can make it there without medical assistance.'

'But *my* doctor,' said Ballantine patiently, 'recommended peanut butter. Martha was sorta doubtful about it, and said that these French cheeses were so great because you could just peel them off and pop them in your mouth. She wanted to know how you were supposed to eat the peanut butter. "With a spoon," I said, "like caviare." ' Ballantine chuckled. 'Well, she had no answer to that,' he concluded triumphantly, 'and I believe she's going to be switching to peanut butter.'

'Somebody ought to warn Sun-Pat,' said Tom.

'Yes, you must be careful,' drawled George, 'or you'll start a run on this butter of yours. Once these Newport people take to something, there's really no stopping them. I remember Brooke Rivers asking me where I had my shirts made, and the next time I ordered some they told me there was a two-year waiting list. They told me there had been a perfectly extraordinary surge in American orders. Well, of course, I knew who that was.'

A waiter came to take the orders and George asked Patrick if he was absolutely sure that he didn't want 'something solid'.

'Absolutely. Nothing solid,' Patrick replied.

'I never knew your father to lose his appetite,' said George.

'No, it was the one thing about him that was reliable.'

'Oh, I wouldn't go that far,' protested George. 'He was an awfully good pianist. Used to keep one up all night,' he explained to the others, 'playing the most spellbinding music.'

Pastiche and parody and hands twisted like old vine stumps, thought Patrick.

'Yes, he could be very impressive at the piano,' he said out loud.

'And in conversation,' George added.

'Mm . . .' said Patrick. 'It depends what you find impressive. Some people don't like uninterrupted rudeness, or so I'm told.'

'Who *are* these people?' asked Tom, looking around the room with mock alarm.

'It is true,' said George, 'that I once or twice had to tell him to stop being quite so argumentative.'

'And what did he do?' asked Ballantine, thrusting his chin forward to get more of his neck out of its tight collar.

'Told me to bugger off,' replied George tersely.

'Hell,' said Ballantine, seeing an opportunity for wisdom and diplomacy. 'You know, people argue about the darnedest things. Why, I spent an entire weekend trying to persuade my wife to dine in Mortimer's the evening we got back to New York. "I'm all Mortimered out," she kept saying, "can't we go someplace else?" Of course she couldn't say where.'

'Of course she couldn't,' said Tom, 'she hasn't seen the inside of another restaurant in fifteen years.'

'All Mortimered out,' repeated Ballantine, his indignation tinged with a certain pride at having married such an original woman.

A lobster, some smoked salmon, a crab salad, and a Bullshot arrived. Patrick lifted the drink greedily to his lips and then froze, hearing the hysterical bellowing of a cow, loud as an abattoir in the muddy liquid of his glass.

'Fuck it,' he murmured, taking a large gulp.

His defiance was soon rewarded with the vivid fantasy that a hoof was trying to kick its way out of his stomach. He remembered, when he was eighteen, writing to his father from a psychiatric ward, trying to explain his reasons for being there, and receiving a short note in reply. Written in Italian, which his father knew he could not understand, it turned out, after some research, to be a quotation from Dante's *Inferno*: 'Consider your descent / You were not made to live among beasts / But to pursue virtue and knowledge.' What had seemed a frustratingly sublime response at the time, struck him with a fresh sense of relevance now that he was listening to the sound of howling, snuffling cattle and felt, or thought he felt, another blow on the inner wall of his stomach.

As his heart rate increased again and a new wave

of sweat prickled his skin, Patrick realised that he was going to be sick.

'Excuse me,' he said, getting up abruptly.

'Are you all right, my dear?' said George.

'I feel rather sick.'

'Perhaps we should get you a doctor.'

'I have the best doctor in New York,' said Ballantine. 'Just mention my name and . . .'

Patrick tasted a bitter surge of bile from his stomach. He swallowed stubbornly and, without time to thank Ballantine for his kind offer, hurried out of the dining room.

On the stairs Patrick forced down a second mouthful of vomit, more solid than the first. Time was running out. Wave after wave of nausea heaved the contents of his stomach into his mouth with increasing velocity. Feeling dizzy, his vision blurred by watering eyes, he fumbled down the corridor, knocking one of the hunting prints askew with his shoulder. By the time he reached the cool marble sanctuary of the lavatories, his cheeks were as swollen as a trumpeter's. A member of the club, admiring himself with that earnestness reserved for mirrors, found that the ordinary annoyance of being interrupted was soon replaced by alarm at being so close to a man who was obviously about to vomit.

Patrick, despairing of reaching the loo, threw up in the basin next to him, turning the taps on at the same time.

'Jesus,' said the member, 'you could have done that in the john.'

'Too far,' said Patrick, throwing up a second time.

'Jesus,' repeated the man, leaving hastily.

Patrick recognised traces of last night's dinner and, with his stomach already empty, knew that he would soon be bringing up that sour yellow bile which gives vomiting its bad name.

To encourage the faster disappearance of the vomit he twirled his finger in the plug-hole and increased the flow of water with his other hand. He longed to gain the privacy of one of the cubicles before he was sick again. Feeling queasy and hot, he abandoned the not yet entirely clean basin and staggered over to one of the mahogany cubicles. He hardly had time to slide the brass lock closed before he was stooped over the bowl of the loo convulsing fruitlessly. Unable to breathe or to swallow, he found himself trying to vomit with even more conviction than he had tried to avoid vomiting a few minutes earlier.

Just when he was about to faint from lack of air he managed to bring up a globule of that yellow bile he had been anticipating with such dread.

'Fucking hell,' he cursed, sliding down the wall.

However often he did it, being sick never lost its power to surprise him.

Shaken by coming so close to choking, he lit a cigarette and smoked it through the bitter slime that coated his mouth. The question now, of course, was whether to take some heroin to help him calm down.

The risk was that it would make him feel even more nauseous.

Wiping the sweat from his hands, he gingerly opened the packet of heroin over his lap, dipped his little finger into it, and sniffed through both nostrils. Not feeling any immediate ill-effects, he repeated the dose.

Peace at last. He closed his eyes and sighed. The others could just fuck off. He wasn't going back. He was going to fold his wings and (he took another sniff) relax. Where he took his smack was his home, and more often than not that was in some stranger's bog.

He was so tired; he really must get some sleep. Get some sleep. Fold his wings. But what if George and the others sent somebody to look for him and they found the sick-spattered basin and hammered on the door of the cubicle? Was there no peace, no resting place? Of course there wasn't. What an absurd question.

CHAPTER ELEVEN

'I'm here to collect the remains of David Melrose,' said Patrick to the grinning young·man with the big jaw and the mop of shiny chestnut hair.

'Mr . . . David . . . Melrose,' he mused, as he turned the pages of a large leather register.

Patrick leant over the edge of the counter, more like a grounded pulpit than a desk, and saw, next to the register, a cheap exercise book marked 'Almost Dead'. That was the file to get on; might as well apply straight away.

Escaping from the Key Club had left him strangely elated. After passing out for an hour in the loo, he had woken refreshed but unable to face the others. Bolting past the doorman like a criminal, he had dashed round the corner to a bar, and then walked on to the funeral parlour. Later he would have to apologise to George. Lie and apologise as he always did or wanted to do after any contact with another human being.

'Yes sir,' said the receptionist brightly, finding the page. 'Mr David Melrose.'

'I have come not to praise him, but to *bury* him,' Patrick declared, thumping the table theatrically.

'Bu-ry him?' stammered the receptionist. 'We under-stood that party was to be cre-mated.'

'I was speaking metaphorically.'

'Metaphorically,' repeated the young man, not quite reassured. Did that mean the customer was going to sue or not?

'Where are the ashes?' asked Patrick.

'I'll go fetch them for you, sir,' said the reception-ist. 'We have you down for a box,' he added, no longer as confident as he'd sounded at first.

'That's right,' said Patrick. 'No point in wasting money on an urn. The ashes are going to be scattered anyway.'

'Right,' said the receptionist with uncertain cheer-fulness.

Glancing sideways he quickly rectified his tone. 'I'll attend to that right away, sir,' he said in an unctuous and artificially loud singsong, setting off promptly towards a door concealed in the panelling.

Patrick looked over his shoulder to find out what had provoked this new eagerness. He saw a tall figure he recognised without immediately being able to place him.

'We're in an industry where the supply and the demand are *bound* to be identical,' quipped this half-familiar man.

Behind him stood the bald, moustachioed director who had led Patrick to his father's corpse the previous afternoon. He seemed to wince and smile at the same time.

'We've got the one resource that's never going to run out,' said the tall man, obviously enjoying himself.

The director raised his eyebrows and flickered his eyes in Patrick's direction.

Of course, thought Patrick, it was that ghastly man he'd met on the plane.

'Goddamn,' whispered Earl Hammer, 'I guess I still got something to learn about PR.' Recognising Patrick, he shouted 'Bobby!' across the chequered marble hall.

'Patrick,' said Patrick.

'Paddy! Of course. That eyepatch was unfamiliar to me. What happened to you anyway? Some lady give you a black eye?' Earl guffawed, pounding over to Patrick's side.

'Just a little inflamation,' said Patrick. 'Can't see properly out of that eye.'

'That's too bad,' said Earl. 'What are you doing here anyhow? When I told you on the plane that I had been diversifying my business interests, I bet you never guessed that I was in the process of acquiring New York's premier funeral parlour.'

'I hadn't guessed that,' confessed Patrick. 'And I don't suppose you guessed that I was coming to collect my father's remains from New York's premier funeral parlour.'

'Hell,' said Earl, 'I'm sorry to hear that. I'll bet he was a fine man.'

'He was perfect in his way,' said Patrick.

'My condolences,' said Earl, with that abrupt solemnity that Patrick recognised from the discussion about Miss Hammer's volleyball prospects.

The receptionist returned with a simple wooden box about a foot long and eight inches high.

'It's so much more compact than a coffin, don't you think?' commented Patrick.

'There's no way of denying that,' Earl replied.

'Do you have a bag?' Patrick asked the receptionist.

'A bag?'

'Yes, a carrier bag, a brown paper bag, that sort of thing.'

'I'll go check that, sir.'

'Paddy,' said Earl, as if he had been giving the matter some thought, 'I want you to have a ten per cent discount.'

'Thank you,' said Patrick, genuinely pleased.

'Don't mention it,' said Earl.

The receptionist returned with a brown paper bag that was already a little crumpled, and Patrick imagined that he'd had to empty out his groceries hastily in order not to fail in front of his employer.

'Perfect,' said Patrick.

'Do we charge for these bags?' asked Earl, and then, before the receptionist could answer, he added, 'Because this one's on me.'

'Earl, I don't know what to say.'

'It's nothing,' said Earl. 'I have a meeting right now, but I would be honoured if you would have a drink with me later.'

'Can I bring my father?' asked Patrick, raising the bag.

'Hell, yes,' said Earl, laughing.

'Seriously, though, I'm afraid I can't. I'm going out to dinner tonight and I have to fly back to England tomorrow.'

'That's too bad.'

'Well, it's a great regret to me,' said Patrick with a wan smile, as he headed quickly for the door.

'Goodbye, old friend,' said Earl, with a big wave.

'Bye now,' said Patrick, flicking up the collar of his overcoat before he ventured into the rush hour street.

In the black-lacquered hall, opposite the opening doors of the elevator, an African mask gawked from a marble-topped console table. The gilded aviary of a Chippendale mirror gave Patrick a last chance to glance with horror at his fabulously ill-looking face before turning to Mrs Banks, Marianne's emaciated mother, who stood vampirishly in the elegant gloom.

Opening her arms so that her black silk dress stretched from her wrists to her knees, like bat's wings, she cocked her head a little to one side and exclaimed with excrutiated sympathy, 'Oh, Patrick, we were so sorry to hear your news.'

161

'Well,' said Patrick, tapping the casket he held under his arm, 'you know how it is: ashes to ashes, dust to dust. What the Lord giveth he taketh away. After what I regard, in this case, as an unnaturally long delay.'

'Is that . . . ?' asked Mrs Banks, staring round-eyed at the brown paper bag.

'My father,' confirmed Patrick.

'I must tell Ogilvy we'll be one more for dinner,' she said with peals of chic laughter. That was Nancy Banks all over, as magazines often pointed out after photographing her drawing room, so daring but so *right*.

'Banquo doesn't eat meat,' said Patrick, putting the box down firmly on the hall table.

Why had he said Banquo? Nancy wondered, in her husky inner voice which, even in the deepest intimacy of her own thoughts, was turned to address a large and fascinated audience. Could he, in some crazy way, feel responsible for his father's death? Because he had wished for it so often in fantasy? God, she had gotten good at this after seventeen years of analysis. After all, as Dr Morris had said when they were talking through their affair, what was an analyst but a former patient who couldn't think of anything better to do? Sometimes she missed Jeffrey. He had let her call him Jeffrey during the 'letting-go process' that had been brought to such an abrupt close by his suicide. Without even a note! Was she really meeting the challenges of life, as Jeffrey had promised? Maybe she was 'incompletely analysed'. It was too dreadful to contemplate.

'Marianne's dying to see you,' she murmured consolingly as she led Patrick into the empty drawing room. He stared at a baroque escritoire cascading with crapulous putti.

'She got a phone call the moment you arrived and couldn't get out of answering it,' she added.

'We have the whole evening . . .' said Patrick. And the whole night, he thought optimistically. The drawing room was a sea of pink lilies, their shining pistils accusing him of lust. He was dangerously obsessed, dangerously obsessed. And his thoughts, like a bob-sleigh walled with ice, would not change their course until he had crashed or achieved his end. He wiped his hands sweatily on his trousers, amazed to have found a preoccupation stronger than drugs.

'Ah, there's Eddy,' exclaimed Nancy.

Mr Banks strode into the room in a chequered lumberjack shirt and a pair of baggy trousers.

'Hello,' he said with his rapid little blur, 'I was tho thorry to hear about your fawther. Marianne says that he was a wemarkable man.'

'You should have heard the remarks,' said Patrick.

'Did you have a very difficult relationship with him?' asked Nancy encouragingly.

'Yup,' Patrick replied.

'When did the twouble stawt?' asked Eddy, settling down on the faded orange velvet of a bow-legged marquise.

'Oh June the ninth, 1906, the day he was born.'

'That early?' smiled Nancy.

'Well, we're not going to resolve the question of whether his problems were congenital or not, at least not before dinner; but even if they weren't, he didn't delay in acquiring them. By all accounts, the moment he could speak he dedicated his new skill to hurting people. By the age of ten he was banned from his grandfather's house because he used to set everyone against each other, cause accidents, force people to do things they didn't want to.'

'You make him sound evil in a rather old-fashioned way. The satanic child,' said Nancy sceptically.

'It's a point of view,' said Patrick. 'When he was around, people were always falling off rocks, or nearly drowning, or bursting into tears. His life consisted of acquiring more and more victims for his malevolence and then losing them again.'

'He must have been charming as well,' said Nancy.

'He was a kitten,' said Patrick.

'But wouldn't we now say that he was just wery disturbed?' asked Eddy.

'So what if we did? When the effect somebody has is destructive enough the cause becomes a theoretical curiosity. There are some very nasty people in the world and it is a pity if one of them is your father.'

'I don't think that people noo so much about how to bring up kids in those days. A lot of parents in your fawther's generation just didn't know how to express their love.'

'Cruelty is the opposite of love,' said Patrick, 'not just some inarticulate version of it.'

'Sounds right to me,' said a husky voice from the doorway.

'Oh, hi,' said Patrick, swivelling around in his chair, suddenly self-conscious in Marianne's presence.

Marianne sailed towards him across the dim drawing room, its floorboards creaking underfoot, and her body tipped forward at a dangerous angle like the figurehead on the prow of a ship.

Patrick rose and wrapped his arms around her with greed and desperation.

'Hey, Patrick,' she said, hugging him warmly. 'Hey,' she repeated soothingly when he seemed reluctant to let go. 'I'm so sorry. Really, really sorry.'

Oh, God, thought Patrick, this is where I want to be buried.

'We were just tawking about how parents sometimes don't know how to express their love,' lisped Eddy.

'Well, I guess I wouldn't know about that,' said Marianne with a cute smile.

Her back as curved as a negress's, she walked towards the drinks tray with awkward and hesitating grace, as if she were a mermaid only recently equipped with human legs, and helped herself to a glass of champagne.

'Does anybody wanna a glass of this,' she stammered, craning her neck forward and frowning slightly, as if the question might contain hidden depths.

Nancy declined. She preferred cocaine. Whatever you said about it, it wasn't fattening. Eddy accepted and Patrick said he wanted whisky.

'Eddy hasn't really gotten over *his* father's death,' said Nancy to nudge the conversation on a little.

'I never really told my fawther how I felt,' explained Eddy, smiling at Marianne as she handed him a glass of champagne.

'Neither did I,' said Patrick. 'Probably just as well in my case.'

'What would you have said?' asked Marianne, fixing him intently with her dark blue eyes.

'I would have said . . . I can't say . . .' Patrick was bewildered and annoyed by having taken the question seriously. 'Never mind,' he mumbled, and poured himself some whisky.

Nancy reflected that Patrick was not really pulling his weight in this conversation.

'They fuck you up. They don't mean to but they do,' she sighed.

'Who says they don't mean to?' growled Patrick.

'Philip Larkin,' said Nancy, with a glassy little laugh.

'But what was it about your father that you couldn't get over?' Patrick asked Eddy politely.

'He was kind of a hero to me. He always noo what to do in any situation, or at least what he wanted to do. He knew how to handle money and women; and when he hooked a three-hundred-pound marlin, the marlin always lost. And when he bid for a picture at auction, he always got it.'

'And when *you* wanted to sell it again you always succeeded,' said Nancy humorously.

'Well, you're *my* hero,' stammered Marianne to her father, 'and I don't want to get over it.'

Fucking hell, thought Patrick, what do these people do all day, write scripts for *The Brady Bunch*? He hated happy families with their mutual encouragement, and their demonstrative affection, and the impression they gave of valuing each other more than other people. It was utterly disgusting.

'Are we going out to dinner together?' Patrick asked Marianne abruptly.

'We could have dinner here.' She swallowed, a little frown clouding her face.

'Would it be frightfully rude to go out?' he insisted. 'I'd like to talk.'

The answer was clearly yes, as far as Nancy was concerned, it would be frightfully rude. Consuela was preparing the scallops this very minute. But in life, as in entertaining, one had to be flexible and graceful and, in this case, some allowances should be made for Patrick's bereavement. It was hard not to be insulted by the implication that she was handling it badly, until one considered that his state of mind was akin to temporary insanity.

'Of course not,' she purred.

'Where shall we go?' asked Patrick.

'Ah . . . there's a small Armenian restaurant I really really like,' Marianne suggested.

'A small Armenian restaurant,' Patrick repeated flatly.

'It's so great,' gulped Marianne.

CHAPTER TWELVE

Under a cerulean dome dotted with dull-gold stars Marianne and Patrick, in a blue velveteen booth of their own, read the plastic-coated menus of the Byzantium Grill. The muffled rumble of a subway train shuddered underfoot and the iced water, always so redundant and so quick to arrive, trembled in the stout ribbed glasses. Everything was shaking, thought Patrick, molecules dancing in the table-top, electrons spinning, signals and sound-waves undulating through his cells, cells shimmering with Country music and police radios, roaring garbage trucks and shattering bottles; his cranium shuddering like a drilled wall, and each sensation Tabasco flicked onto his soft grey flesh.

A passing waiter kicked Patrick's box of ashes, looked round and apologised. Patrick refused his offer to 'check that for you' and slid the box further under the table with his feet.

Death should express the deeper being rather than represent the occasion for a new role. Who had said that? The terror of forgetting. And yet here was his father being kicked around by a waiter. A new role, definitely a new role.

Perhaps Marianne's body would enable him to forget his father's corpse, perhaps it contained a junction where his obsession with his father's death and his own dying could switch tracks and hurtle towards its new erotic destination with all of its old morbid *élan*. What should he say? What could he say?

Angels, of course, made love without obstruction of limb or joint, but in the sobbing frustration of human love-making, the exasperating substitution of ticklishness for interfusion, and the ever-renewed drive to pass beyond the mouth of the river to the calm lake where we were conceived, there would have been, thought Patrick, as he pretended to read the menu but in fact fixed his eyes on the green velvet that barely contained Marianne's breasts, an adequate expression of the failure of words to convey the confusion and intensity he felt in the wake of his father's death.

Besides, not having fucked Marianne was like not having read the *Iliad* – something else he had been meaning to do for a long time.

Like a sleeve caught in some implacable and uncomprehending machine, his need to be understood had become lodged in her blissful but dangerously indifferent body. He would be dragged through a crushing obsession and spat out the other end without her pulse flickering or her thoughts wandering from their chosen paths.

Instead of her body saving him from his father's corpse, their secrets would become intertwined; half the horizon formed by his broken lip, half by her unbroken lips. And this vertiginous horizon, like an encircling waterfall, would suck him away from safety, as if he stood on a narrow column of rock watching the dragging water turn smooth around him, seeming still as it turned to fall, falling everywhere.

Jesus, thought Marianne, why had she agreed to have dinner with this guy? He read the menu like he was staring at a ravine from a high bridge. She couldn't bear to ask him another question about his father, but it seemed wrong to make him talk about anything else.

The whole evening could turn into a major drag. He was in some drooling state between loathing and desire. It was enough to make a girl feel guilty about being so attractive. She tried to avoid it, but she had spent too much of her life sitting opposite hangdog men she had nothing in common with, their eyes burning with reproach, and the conversation long-congealed and mouldy, like something from way way *way* back in the icebox, something you must have been crazy to have bought in the first place.

Vine leaves and houmous, grilled lamb, rice and red wine. At least she could eat. The food here was really good. Simon had brought her here first. He had a gift for finding the best Armenian restaurants in any city in the world. Simon was so so clever. He

171

wrote poems about swans and ice and stars, and it was tough to know what he was trying to say, because they were so indirect without really being very suggestive. But he was a genius of *savoir-faire*, especially in the Armenian restaurant department. One day Simon had said to her in his faintly Brooklyn stammer, 'Some people have certain emotions. I don't.' Just like that. No swans, no ice, no stars, nothing.

They had made love once and she had tried to absorb the essence of his impudent, elusive genius, but when it was over he had gone into the bathroom to write a poem, and she'd lain in bed feeling like an ex-swan. Of course it was wrong to want to change people, but what else could you possibly want to do with them?

Patrick aroused a reforming zeal akin to carpet bombing. Those slit eyes and curling lips, that arrogant way he arched one of his eyebrows, the stooped, near-foetal posture, the stupid self-destructive melodrama of his life – which of these could not be cheerfully cast aside? But then what would be left if you threw out the rotten stuff? It was like trying to imagine bread without the dough.

There he was, drooling at her again. The green velvet dress was obviously a big hit. It made her angry to think of Debbie, who was ragged and crazy with love of this sleazeball (Marianne had made the mistake of calling him a 'temporary aberration' at the beginning, but Debbie had forgiven her now that she

172

wished it was true), of Debbie being rewarded with this would-be infidelity, no doubt as generalised as his insatiable appetite for drugs.

The trouble with doing something you didn't like was that it made you conscious of all the things that you should be doing instead. Even going to the movies for the first performance of the afternoon failed to provoke the sense of burning urgency she felt right now. The untaken photographs, the call of the dark room, the sting of unwritten thank-you letters which had left her untroubled until now, all crowded in and gave an even more desperate air to the conversation she was having with Patrick.

Condemned to the routine of dismissing men, she sometimes wished (especially tonight) that she didn't arouse emotions she could do nothing to satisfy. Naturally a *tiny* part of her wanted to save them, or at least stop them trying so hard.

Patrick had to acknowledge that the conversation was going pretty badly. Every line he threw to the quayside slipped back heavily into the filthy harbour. She might as well have had her back turned to him, but then nothing excited him more than a turned back. Each mute appeal, disguised by a language as banal as it was possible to imagine, made him more conscious of how little experience he had of saying what he meant. If he could speak to her in another voice, or with another intention – to deceive or to ridicule, for example – then he could wake from this tongue-tied nightmare.

Thick, black and sweet, the coffee arrived. Time was running out. Couldn't she see what was going on? Couldn't she read between the lines? And so what if she could? Perhaps she liked to see him suffer. Perhaps she didn't even like that about him.

Marianne yawned and complained of tiredness. All the signs are good at this point, thought Patrick sarcastically. She's dying for it, *dying* for it. Yes means yes, maybe means yes, perhaps means yes, and no of course means yes as well. He knew how to read women like an open book.

Outside in the street, Marianne kissed him good-bye, sent her love to Debbie, and grabbed a cab.

Patrick stormed down Madison Avenue with his father on his arm. The brown paper bag occasionally crashed into a passer-by who was unwise enough not to get out of the way.

By the time he reached Sixty-First Street, Patrick realised that it was the first time he had been alone with his father for more than ten minutes without being buggered, hit, or insulted. The poor man had had to confine himself to blows and insults for the last fourteen years, and insults alone for the last six.

The tragedy of old age, when a man is too weak to hit his own child. No wonder he had died. Even his rudeness had been flagging towards the end, and he had been forced to introduce a note of repulsive self-pity to ward off any counter-attack.

'Your trouble,' snarled Patrick, as he swept past the doorman of his hotel, 'is that you're mentally ill.'

'You mustn't say those things to your poor old father,' he murmured, shaking imaginary heart pills into a bunched and twisted palm.

Bastard. Nobody should do that to anybody else. Never mind, never tell.

Stop thinking about it right now.

'Right now,' said Patrick out loud.

Death and destruction. Buildings swallowed by flame as he passed. Windows shattering at a glance. An inaudible jugular-bursting scream. No prisoners.

'Death and destruction,' he muttered. Christ, he was really anxious now, really very *fucking anxious*.

Patrick imagined sliding a chain-saw through the neck of the lift operator. Wave after wave of shame and violence, ungovernable shame and violence.

If thy head offend thee, cut it off. Incinerate it and trample it into ash. No prisoners, no pity. Tamburlaine's black tent. My favourite colour! It's so chic.

'Which floor, sir?'

What are you staring at, fuckface?

'Thirty-nine.'

Steps. Over-associative. Over-accelerated.

Sedation. Scalpel. Patrick flicked out his hand. Anaesthetic first, surely, Doctor?

Surely: the adverb of a man without an argument. Scalpel first, anaesthetic afterwards. The Dr Death Method. You know it makes sense.

Whose idea was it to put him on the thirty-ninth floor? What were they trying to do? Drive him mad?

Hide under the sofa. Must hide under the sofa.

175

Nobody can find me there. What if nobody finds me there? What if they do?

Patrick burst into the room, dropped the brown paper bag, and threw himself onto the floor. He rolled over towards the sofa, lay on his back, and tried to squirm underneath the skirt of the sofa.

What was he doing? He was going mad. Can't get under the sofa any more. Too big now. Six foot two. No longer a child.

Fuck that. He lifted the sofa into the air and insinuated his body underneath it, lowering it again onto his chest.

And he lay there in his overcoat and his eyepatch, with the sofa covering him up to his neck, like a coffin built for a smaller man.

Dr Death: 'This is just the sort of episode we had hoped to avoid. Scalpel. Anaesthetic.' Patrick flicked out his hand.

Not that again. Quickly, quickly, a fix of smack.

More of the speed capsules must be dissolving in his stomach. There was an explanation for everything.

'There isn't a bin in the world that wouldn't take you for free,' he sighed in the voice of an affectionate but dishonest hospital matron, as he wriggled from under the sofa and got up slowly to his knees.

He slipped out of his now rather crumpled and fluff-covered overcoat and crawled towards the box of ashes on all fours, watching it carefully as if it might pounce.

How could he get into the box? Get into the box, take out the ashes and empty them down the loo. What better resting place could there be for his father than a New York sewer, among the albino wild life and tons of shit?

He examined the bevelled cedarwood for a gap or a screw which would enable him to prise the casket open, but only found a thin gold plaque taped to the seamless base in a tiny plastic bag.

In fury and frustration, Patrick leapt to his feet and jumped up and down on the box. It was made of sturdier wood than he had imagined and withstood the assault without a creak. Could he order a chain-saw from Room Service? He remembered no mention of it on the menu.

Drop it out of the window and watch it shatter on the pavement? He would probably kill someone without denting the box.

With one last effort Patrick kicked the impregnable casket across the floor, where it hit the metal waste-paper basket with a hollow clang and came to a rest.

With admirable swiftness and efficiency, Patrick prepared and administered an injection of heroin.

His eyelids clicked closed. And half opened again, cool and inert.

If only it could always be like this, the calm of the initial hit. But even in this voluptuous Caribbean tranquillity there were too many snapped trees and flayed roofs to let him relax. There was always an argument to win, or a feeling to fight off. He glanced at the box. Observe Everything. Always think for yourself. Never let other people make important decisions for you.

Patrick scratched himself lazily. Well, at least he didn't care so much.

CHAPTER THIRTEEN

Patrick had tried to sleep, but tattered rags of speed still trailed through his consciousness and kept him charging forward. He rubbed his eye compulsively, obsessed with the stye that tickled his eyeball with each blink. The jelly they had given him at the pharmacy was of course completely useless. Nevertheless, he squirted a large amount into his eye and his vision blurred like a greased camera. The eyepatch had left a diagonal dent across his forehead, and he only stopped rubbing his eye to scratch the dent with the same desperate irritation. He wanted to scratch out his eye and peel off his face to end the terrible itchiness that had erupted from his failed attempt to sleep, but knew that it was only the surface play of a more fundamental unease: itching powder in the first pair of nappies, sniggering faces around the hospital cot.

He rolled off the bed, loosening his tie. The room was stiflingly hot, but he loathed the meat-locker cold of the air-conditioning. What was he, a carcass on a hook? A corpse in a morgue? Better not to ask.

It was time to check his drugs, to review his troops and see what chance he had of making it through another night and getting onto the plane the next morning at nine-thirty.

He sat down at the desk, taking the heroin and pills out of his coat pockets and the coke from an envelope in his suitcase. He had about one and a half out of the seven grams of coke, about a fifth of a gram of heroin, one Quaalude and one Black Beauty. If he wasn't going to sleep but abandon himself to shooting coke, then there was only enough for two or three hours. It was eleven o'clock now and even with exemplary self-restraint, whatever that was, he would be left with the agony of the come-down in the deadest part of the night. There was enough heroin, just. He was still okay from the fix he'd had after dinner. If he had one at three in the morning and one just before getting on the plane, he'd be able to last until he got to Johnny Hall's. Thank God for Concorde. On the other hand, more coke meant more smack to control the danger of heart attack and insanity, and so he should try to avoid scoring again, or he'd be too out of it for Customs.

The sensible thing to do was to try to divide the coke into two halves, taking the first now and the second after he had gone out to a nightclub or bar. He would try to stay out until three and take the amphetamines just before returning, so that the lift from the speed would cushion the coke come-down after the second bout of fixing. The Black Beauty had about a fifteen-hour life, or maybe a twelve-hour life on the second day, which meant that the effect would be wearing off at about three in the afternoon New York time – eight o'clock London time: just when he could expect to arrive at Johnny's and get some more gear.

Brilliant! He really ought to be in charge of a multinational company or a wartime army to find an outlet for these planning skills. The Quaalude was a free-floating agent. He could use it to cope with the boredom of the plane flight, or give it to some chick in the Mud Club so as to get her into bed. The incident with Marianne had left him bruised, like a bad Dry Martini. He wanted to strike back at the female sex and also to satisfy the desires that Marianne had inflamed.

So, he could have a fix of coke now. Yes, yes, yes. He wiped his clammy hands on his trousers and began to prepare the solution. His bowels loosened at the thought, and all the longing that a man bestows on a woman who is betraying him and whose betrayal deepens his longing and enslaves him as her fidelity never could, all the impatience and desperation of waiting while flowers wither in his hands, assailed him. It was love, there was no other word for it.

Like an incompetent bullfighter who cannot find the angle for a kill, Patrick stabbed at his veins without bringing blood into the barrel. Trying to calm himself down, he breathed deeply and reintroduced the needle into his arm, moving it slowly clockwise to find an angle that would break the wall of the vein without going through the other side. As he made this arc, he teased the plunger upwards with his thumb.

At last a small thread of blood galloped into the barrel and circled round. Patrick held the syringe as still as possible and pushed down the plunger. The mechanism was stiff and he immediately pulled the plunger back. He felt a sharp pain in his arm. He had lost the vein! He lad lost the fucking vein. He was in the muscle. There was only about twenty seconds before the blood coagulated and then he would be shooting a heart-arresting clot into his bloodstream. But if he didn't shoot it up the fix would be ruined. Heat could miraculously reliquify the blood in a solution of heroin, but it would spoil the coke. Almost weeping with frustration, Patrick didn't know whether to push deeper or withdraw the needle. Taking a gamble, he retracted the syringe slightly and flattened it at the same time. More blood curled into the barrel and, with hysterical gratitude, he pushed the plunger down as hard as he could. It was insane to shoot up so quickly, but he couldn't take the risk of the blood coagulating. When he tried to draw the plunger back a second time to make sure he got all the coke that was still lurking in the barrel, he found the mechanism stuck and realised that he had slipped out of the vein again.

He whipped the spike out of his arm and, struggling against a flood of promiscuous lucidity, tried to fill the barrel with water before the blood dried. His hands shook so badly that the syringe clinked on the side of the glass. Jesus, it was strong. Once he had sucked in the water, he put the syringe down, too high to flush it out.

Clasping his arm so that the fist was couched under his chin, he rocked back and forth on the edge of his chair and tried to disperse the pain. But he could not shake off the sense of intimate violation that came with every botched fix. The walls of his veins were perforated again and again by the thin steel he had stuck into them, torturing his body to gratify his mind.

The coke was marauding through his system, like a pack of white wolves, spreading terror and destruction. Even the brief euphoria of the rush had been eclipsed by the fear that he had shot up a blood clot. Next time he would inject himself in the back of his hand where he could still see the veins clearly. The good old-fashioned pain of puncturing that tough skin and probing the tiny delicate bones, was less spooky than the horror of missed invisible veins. At least he wasn't fixing in his groin. Gouging around unsuccessfully among those elusive veins could make one question the whole intravenous method of absorbing drugs.

In fact, it was at times like this, in the wake of missed veins, overdoses, minor heart attacks, and fainting fits, that his vicious addiction to needles, quite apart from drugs, made him want to bend spikes and post syringes down drains. It was only the certainty that these quarrels were always lost and merely committed him to the tedious search for new works, or the humiliation of fishing the old ones out from under the wet Kleenexes, slimy yoghurt pots, and limp potato peel of the bin liner, that prevented Patrick from destroying his syringes straight away.

This needle fever had a psychological life of its own. What better way to be at once the fucker and the fucked, the subject and the object, the scientist and the experiment, trying to set the spirit free by enslaving the body? What other form of self-division was more expressive than the androgynous embrace of an injection, one arm locking the needle into the other, enlisting pain into the service of pleasure and forcing pleasure back into the service of pain?

He had injected whisky, watching his burnt vein turn black under the skin, just to satisfy the needle fever. He had dissolved cocaine in Perrier, because the tap was too far away for his imperious desire. Brain like a bowl of Rice Crispies – snap! crackle! pop! – and a disturbing effervescence in the valves of his heart. He had woken up after passing out for thirty hours, the syringe, still half full of smack, hanging loosely from his arm, and started again, with that cold annihilating will, the ritual that had nearly killed him.

Patrick could not help wondering, after his failure to capture Marianne, if a syringe would not have been a better intermediary than his conversation. It made him sentimental to think of Natasha saying in her hoarse whisper, 'Baby, you're so good, you always hit the vein,' a trickle of dark blood flowing from her pale arm as it dangled over the edge of the chair.

He'd shot her up the first time they'd met. She had sat on the sofa with her knees raised, and proffered her arm trustingly. He sat beside her on the floor, and when he gave her the fix, her knees fell open, gathering light in the heavy folds of her black silk trousers, and he was overwhelmed with tenderness as she fell back and sighed, her eyes closed and her face glowing, 'Too much . . . pleasure . . . too much.'

What was sex next to this compassionate violence? Only this violence could break open a world constrained by the hidden cameras of conscience and vanity.

After that, their relationship had decayed from injection to intercourse, from dazzled recognition to chat. Still, thought Patrick, dazed by the solid-looking objects around him, as he got up from his chair and out of his trance, he had to believe that somewhere out there was a girl willing to trade her body for a couple of drinks and a Quaalude. And he was going to begin his search at the Mud Club. After one more quick fix.

* * *

An hour later, Patrick managed with some difficulty to leave the hotel. He sprawled in the back of the cab as it rumbled downtown. Those pencils of steel, chrome fans, and crystal towers that seemed to burst like pure soprano notes from a primadonna's hideous, pock-marked face, were muffled by darkness. Cross-word puzzles of lit and unlit offices slipped by clue-lessly. Two lit offices down – call it 'no' – and five across. Five-letter word beginning with 'o'. Oran . . . one . . . order. Call it order. No order. The building disappeared in the back window. Did everyone play this game? The land of the free and the home of the brave, where people only did some-thing if everyone else did too. Had he already thought that? Had he already said that?

As usual, there was a crowd outside the Mud Club. Patrick slipped to the front where two black men and a fat, bearded white man stood behind a twisted red cord and decided who to let in. He greeted the boun-cers in a tired drawl. They always let him in. Perhaps it was because he assumed that they would; or because he didn't really care if they did; or, of course, because he looked rich and likely to order a lot of drinks.

Patrick went straight upstairs where, instead of the live music that was blaring from a small stage on the ground floor, tapes played continuously while videos of spectacular but familiar events – time-lapse flowers suddenly blossoming, Hitler thumping the podium at Nuremberg and then embracing himself in an ecstasy of approval, early attempts at human flight crashing, disintegrating and plummeting from bridges – radiated from a dozen television screens into every angle of the dark room. Just before he stepped inside, a slim sulky girl with short white hair and violet contact lenses slipped passed him down the stairs. Dressed all in black, her white make-up and discontented but symmetrical features made her look like a junkie doll. She even had a black silk tourniquet around her thin bicep. Sweet! He watched her. She was not leaving, just switching rooms. He would check her out later.

The Talking Heads pulsed from every speaker. 'The centre is missing,' gasped David Byrne, and Patrick could not help agreeing with him. How did they know exactly what he was feeling? It was spooky.

A shot of a cheetah chasing an antelope through the African bush flickered onto all the screens at once. Patrick pressed himself against the wall as if he had been thrown back by the centrifugal force of a spinning room. He felt waves of weakness and exhaustion when the real state of his body broke through the guard of drugs. The last fix of coke had petered out on the journey down and he might have to take that Black Beauty sooner than scheduled.

The antelope was brought down in a cloud of dust. Its legs twitched for a while as the cheetah ate into its neck. At first the event seemed to shatter and

187

dissipate among all the screens, and then, as the shot closed in, the kill multiplied and gathered force.

The room still seemed to Patrick to be throwing him backwards, as if rejection and exclusion, the companions of any social contact, had been turned into a physical force. Sometimes the startling contentment of a smack rush caused him to believe that the universe was indifferent rather than hostile, but such a touching faith was bound to be betrayed and seemed especially remote now, as he rested with flattened palms against the wall of the room.

Naturally, he still thought of himself in the third person, as a character in a book or a movie, but at least it was still the third person singular. 'They' hadn't come to get him yet tonight, the bacteria of voices that had taken over the night before. In the presence of the absence, in the absence of the presence, Tweedledee and Tweedledum. Life imitating bad literary criticism. Dis/inte/gration. Exhausted and febrile. Business as usual. Funny business as usual.

Like a man in the spinning barrel of a funfair, Patrick unglued himself laboriously from the wall. Under the shimmering blue light of the televisions, cool customers sprawled uncomfortably on the bench of soft grey cushions that ran around the edge of the room. Patrick walked towards the bar with the care of a driver trying to convince a policeman that he is sober.

'Doctor said his liver looked like a relief map of

the Rockies,' said a thick-necked, jocular man leaning on the bar.

Patrick winced and immediately felt a needle-sharp twinge in his side. Absurdly suggestible, must try to calm down. In a parody of detachment, he swivelled his eyes around the room with the small staccato movements of a predatory lizard.

Sprawling on the cushion nearest to the bar was a guy in a red and yellow kilt, a studded belt, army boots, a black leather jacket and thunderbolt earrings. He looked as if he'd had too many Tuinals. Patrick thought of the black flash of the Tuinal rush, burning the arm like scouring powder; strictly an emergency measure. The look struck him as outmoded; after all, it was six years since the punk summer of '76 when he'd sat on the fire escape at school in the sweltering heat, smoking joints, listening to 'White Riot', and shouting 'destroy' over the rooftops. Next to the kilted punk were two nervous New Jersey secretaries perched on the edge of their seats in tight trousers that cut into their soft bellies. They transferred red lipstick to their all-white cigarette butts with promising zeal, but were too hideous to be considered for the task of consoling him for Marianne's indifference. With his back slightly turned to them, a commodity broker in a dark suit (or was he an art dealer?) was talking to a man who compensated for his near-baldness with a long wispy curtain of grey hair emerging from the last productive follicles at the back of his skull. They looked as if they were keeping in touch

189

with the desperate state of youth, checking out the new wave kids, spotting the latest inflections of rebellious fashion.

On the other side of the room, a pretty girl with the ever-popular poor look, a black sweater over a simple second-hand skirt, held hands with a man in a T-shirt and jeans. They stared obediently at one of the TV screens, two glasses of beer at their feet. Beyond them, a group of three people talked excitedly. One man in a cobalt-blue suit and thin tie, and another in a primary-red suit and thin tie, bracketed a hook-nosed girl with long black hair and a pair of leather jodhpurs. From the far reaches of the room, Patrick could make out the gleam of chains.

Hopeless, completely hopeless. The only remotely pretty girl in the room was physically linked to another man. They weren't even having an argument. It was disgusting.

He checked his pockets again, crossing himself devoutly. The smack, the speed, the cash, and the Quaalude. One could never be too paranoid – or could one? The coke was back in the hotel with the credit cards. He ordered a bourbon on the rocks, fished out the Black Beauty, and swallowed it with the first gulp. Two hours ahead of schedule, but never mind. Rules were made to be broken. Which meant, if that was a rule, that sometimes they should be observed. Mind sputtering on. Circular thinking. So tired.

A shot of David Bowie sitting drunkenly in front

of a serried bank of television screens flickered onto the club's television screens, only to be replaced by the famous shot of Orson Welles walking through the hall of mirrors in Charles Foster Kane's Floridian castle. Multiplying images of multiplication.

'I suppose you think that's clever,' sighed Patrick, like a disappointed schoolmaster.

'I'm sorry?'

Patrick turned around. It was a man with the curtain of long grey hair.

'Just talking to myself,' muttered Patrick. 'I was thinking that the images on the screen were empty and out of control.'

'Maybe they are intended to be images about emptiness,' said the man solemnly. 'I think that's something the kids are very much in touch with right now.'

'How can you be in touch with emptiness?' asked Patrick.

'By the way, my name's Alan. Two Beck's,' he said to the waiter. 'What's yours?'

'Bourbon.'

'I mean your name.'

'Oh, eh, Patrick.'

'Hi.' Alan extended his hand. Patrick shook it reluctantly. 'What are headlights flaring on the road?' asked Alan as if it were a riddle.

Patrick shrugged his shoulders.

'Headlights flaring on the road,' Alan replied with admirable calm.

'That's a relief,' said Patrick.

'Everything in life is a symbol of itself.'

'That's what I was afraid of,' said Patrick, 'but luckily words are too slippery to communicate that.'

'They must communicate that,' Alan affirmed. 'It's like when you're screwing you gotta think of the person you're with.'

'I suppose so,' said Patrick sceptically, 'as long as you put them in a different situation.'

'If the screens here show other ways of making images, other screens, mirrors, cameras, you can tell that self-reflection emptiness or you can call it honesty. It announces that it can only announce itself.'

'But what about Batman?' said Patrick. 'That's not about the nature of the television medium.'

'At some level it is.'

'Somewhere below the Batcave.'

'That's right,' said Alan encouragingly, 'somewhere below the Batcave. That's what a lot of the kids feel: the cultural emptiness.'

'I'll take your word for it,' said Patrick.

'*I* happen to think that there's still news of Being worth telling,' said Alan, picking up the bottles of Beck's. 'Whitman's love is more precious than money,' he beamed.

Fucking hell, thought Patrick.

'Do you want to join us?'

'No, in fact I was just going,' said Patrick. 'Frightfully bad jet lag.'

'Okay,' said Alan unperturbed. 'So long.'

'Bye now.'

Patrick drained his glass of bourbon to convince Alan that he was really leaving, and headed for the downstairs room.

He really wasn't doing too well. Not only had he failed to pick up a chick, but he'd had to ward off this loony faggot. What a pick-up line, 'Whitman's love is more precious than money.' Patrick let out a short burst of laughter on the stairs. At least down here he might be able to track down that violet-eyed punk. He had to have her. She was definitely the lucky woman destined to share his hotel bed for the last few hours before he left the country.

The atmosphere downstairs was very different from the carpeted bar above. On the stage, musicians in black T-shirts and torn jeans produced a heavily strumming wall of sound which the lead singer's voice tried unsuccessfully to scale. The long bare room, once a warehouse, had no decorations or fancy lights, only a heroic sense of its own rawness. In this loud darkness, Patrick made out blue and pink spiked hair, zebra, leopard and tiger prints, tight black trousers and pointy shoes, exotics and tramps leaning against the walls sniffing powders, solitary dancers with closed eyes and nodding heads, robotic couples, and small groups of jumping and crashing bodies nearer the stage.

Patrick stood on tiptoe trying to find the violet-eyed junkie doll. She was nowhere to be seen, but he soon became distracted by the back of a blonde girl in a home-made chiffon dress and a black leather jacket. Wandering casually past her he glanced around. 'You must be fucking joking,' he muttered vehemently. He felt angry and betrayed, as if her face were a broken promise.

How could he have been so disloyal? He was after the violet-eyed junkie doll. Debbie had once screamed at him in the middle of an argument, 'Do you know what love is, Patrick? Do you have the faintest idea?' And he'd said wearily, 'How many guesses do I get?'

Patrick doubled back and, checking from side to side, weaved his way across the room and took up a position against the wall.

There she was! With her back to a column and her hands behind her, as if she were tied to a stake, she looked up at the musicians with reverent curiosity. Patrick concentrated madly and imagined her sliding across the floor towards the magnetic field of his chest and stomach. Frowning ferociously, he cast a neurone net over her body and hauled her in like a heavy catch. He whipped mental lassoes around the column she stood beside, and brought her staggering across the floor like a bound slave. Finally, he closed his eyes, took flight, and projected his desire through the room, covering her neck and breasts with kisses.

When he opened his eyes she was gone. Maybe he should have tried conversation. He looked around him indignantly. Where the hell was she? His psychic powers were failing, even though the resurgence of the speed was giving his incompetence a renewed intensity.

He must have her. He must have her, or someone else. He needed contact, skin to skin, muscle to muscle. Above all, he needed the oblivious moment of penetration when, for a second, he could stop thinking about himself. Unless, as too often happened, the appearance of intimacy unleashed a further disembodiment and a deeper privacy. Never mind that. Even if sex sentenced him to an exile which, on top of the usual melancholy, contained the additional irritation of another person's dumb reproach, the conquest was bound to be exhilarating. Or was it? Who was left to him? Beautiful women were always with someone, unless you happened to catch them in the split second between inconsolable loss and consolation, or in the taxi that was taking them from their principal lover to one of the secondary ones. And if you had a beautiful woman, they always kept you waiting, kept you doubting, because it was the only time they could be sure that you were thinking about them.

Having worked himself up into a state of some bitterness, Patrick strode over to the bar.

'Jack Daniel's on the rocks,' he said to the barman.

As he drew back, Patrick checked the girl to his left. She was slightly plump, dark-haired and marginally pretty. She looked back at him steadily, a good sign.

'Aren't you hot in that coat?' she asked. 'It is May, you know.'

'Incredibly hot,' Patrick admitted with a half-smile, 'but I'd feel flayed without it.'

'It's like a defence mechanism,' said the girl.

'Yes,' drawled Patrick, feeling that she had not captured the full subtlety and poignancy of his overcoat. 'What's your name?' he asked as casually as possible.

'Rachel.'

'Mine's Patrick. Can I offer you a drink?' Christ, he sounded like a parody of someone making conversation. Everything had taken on a threatening or facetious aspect that made it harder than ever to climb down from the position of an observer. Perhaps she would experience the crushing dullness as a reassuring ritual.

'Sure. I'd like a beer. A Dos Esquis.'

'Fine,' said Patrick, catching the barman's attention. 'So what kind of work do you do?' he went on, practically vomiting at the effort of making ordinary conversation and feigning an interest in somebody else.

'I work in a gallery.'

'Really?' said Patrick, hoping he sounded impressed. He seemed to have lost all control over his voice.

'Yeah, but I really wanna start a gallery of my own.'

Here we go again, thought Patrick. The waiter

196

who thinks he's an actor, the actor who thinks he's a director, the taxi-driver who thinks he's a philosopher. All the signs are good at this point, the deal is about to happen, there's a lot of interest from the record companies . . . a city full of phoney aggressive fantasists and, of course, a few genuinely unpleasant people with power.

'Only, I need the financial backing,' she sighed.

'Why do you want to start out on your own?' he asked, concerned and yet encouraging.

'I don't know if you're familiar with Neo-Objective Art, but I think it's going to be really major,' said Rachel. 'I know a lot of the artists and I'd like to get their careers started while everybody else is still ignoring them.'

'I'm sure that won't be for long.'

'That's why I gotta move quickly.'

'I'd love to see some Neo-Objective Art,' said Patrick earnestly.

'I could arrange that,' said Rachel, looking at him in a new light. Was this the financial backing she had been waiting for? His overcoat might be weird, but it looked expensive. It might be kinda cool to have an eccentric English backer who wasn't going to breathe down her neck.

'I do a little collecting,' Patrick lied. 'By the way, would you like a Quaalude?'

'I don't really do drugs,' said Rachel, wrinkling her nose.

'Neither do I,' said Patrick. 'I just happen to have

one floating around. Somebody gave it to me ages ago.'

'I don't need to get high to have fun,' said Rachel coolly.

She's on for it, she's definitely on for it, thought Patrick. 'You're so right,' he said, 'it spoils the magic – makes people unreal.' His heartbeat accelerated; he'd better clinch the deal. 'Do you want to come back to my hotel? I'm staying at the Pierre.'

The Pierre, thought Rachel; all the signs were good. 'Sure,' she smiled.

CHAPTER FOURTEEN

Two-thirty according to the clock next to the St Christopher medallion. That gave him about five hours. More than enough, more than a lifetime's worth of conversation with Rachel. He smiled at her vaguely. What could he tell her? That his father had just died? That he was a drug addict? That he was leaving for the airport in five hours? That his girlfriend really wouldn't mind? He certainly didn't want to ask her any more questions about herself. Nor did he want to hear her views on Nicaragua.

'I'm feeling kinda hungry,' said Rachel uneasily.

'Hungry?'

'Yeah, I got this craving for chili.'

'Well, I'm sure we can get you some on Room Service,' said Patrick, who knew perfectly well that there was no chili on the Pierre's all-night menu and would have disapproved if there had been.

'But there's this diner where they make like the greatest chili in the entire world,' said Rachel, sitting up eagerly. 'I *really* wanna go there.'

'Right,' said Patrick patiently. 'What's the address?'

'Eleventh Avenue and Thirty-Eighth.'

'I'm sorry about this,' said Patrick to the driver, 'we've changed our minds. Could we go to Eleventh Avenue and Thirty-Eighth Street instead?'

'Eleventh and Thirty-Eighth?' repeated the driver.

'Yup.'

The diner was a ribbed silver caravan with TRY OUR FAMOUS CHILI AND TACOS in red neon outside. It was an offer that Rachel could not resist. A green neon chili flashed cutely next to a yellow sombrero.

When the giant oval plate arrived loaded with chili-flavoured minced meat, refried beans, guacamole and sour cream, topped with bright orange cheddar and accompanied by speckled ochre tortilla shells, Patrick lit a cigarette in the hope of drawing a veil of thin blue smoke over the pungent heap of spicy food. He took another sip of insipid coffee and sat back as far as possible in the corner of the red plastic bench. Rachel was clearly a nervous overeater, stuffing herself before he stuffed her, or perhaps, very persuasively, trying to put him off sex altogether by wreaking havoc on her digestive system, and saturating her breath with the torrid stench of cheese and chili.

'Uh-hum,' said Rachel appreciatively, 'I love this food.'

Patrick raised an eyebrow slightly but made no comment.

She piled the chili into the tortilla, smeared some guacamole on top and patted down the sour cream with the back of her fork. Finally, she took a pinch of cheddar between her fingers and sprinkled it on top.

The tortilla flopped open and chili flooded onto her chin. Giggling, she lifted it with her index finger and forced it back into her mouth.

'Delicioso,' she commented.

'It looks disgusting,' said Patrick sullenly.

'You should try some.'

She stooped over the plate and found ingenious angles from which to snap at the collapsing tortilla.

Patrick rubbed his eye. It was itching wildly again. He stared out of the window but was drawn back into the arena of its reflections. The tulip-red bar stools on their chrome stems, the hatch into the kitchen, the old man hunched over a cup of coffee and, of course, Rachel like a pig in a trough. It reminded him of the famous painting by whatshisname. Memory getting burnt out. The terror of forgetting everything. Hooper . . . Hopper. Got it. Life in the old dog.

'Finished?' asked Patrick.

'They make a great Banana Split here,' said Rachel saucily, still chomping her last mouthful of chili.

'Well, don't restrain yourself,' said Patrick. 'Will one be enough?'

'Don't you want one too?'

'No, I do not,' said Patrick pompously.

Soon a long glass dish arrived on which scoops of chocolate, vanilla and strawberry ice cream were bracketed by the two halves of a banana, buried under rippling waves of whipped cream and decorated with beads of pink and green candy. Red maraschino cherries ran down the centre like a row of clown's buttons.

Patrick's leg twitched up and down involuntarily as he watched Rachel exhume bits of banana from the mound of brightly coloured creams.

'I've given up dairy products,' she said, 'but I allow myself these binges sometimes.'

'So it seems,' said Patrick stiffly.

He was overcome with loathing and contempt. The girl was completely out of control. Whereas drugs were at least amenable to advertising: life on the edge, exploring the inner Congo, the heart of darkness, outstaring death, returning with the scars and medals of a haunting knowledge, Coleridge, Baudelaire, Leary . . . ; and even if this advertising seemed horribly false to anyone who had taken drugs at all seriously, it wasn't possible even to pretend that there was anything heroic about an eating problem. And yet there was something unsettlingly familiar about Rachel's obsessive greed and ridiculous dishonesty.

'Can we go now?' snapped Patrick.

'Yeah, okay,' said Rachel timidly.

He ordered the check, threw down a twenty-dollar bill before it arrived, and wriggled out of the booth. Another fucking taxi drive, he thought.

★   ★   ★

'I feel kinda nau-tious,' complained Rachel, as they went up in the hotel elevator.

'I'm not surprised,' said Patrick severely, '*I* feel nauseous and I was only watching.'

'Hey, you're pretty hos-tel.'

'I'm sorry,' said Patrick, 'I'm awfully tired.' Better not lose her now.

'Me too,' said Rachel.

Patrick unlocked the door, and switched on the lights.

'Sorry about the mess.'

'You should see my apartment.'

'Maybe I will,' said Patrick, 'and all that Neo-Objective Art.'

'Definitely,' said Rachel. 'Can I use the bathroom?'

'Of course.'

Time to mix a quick fix, thought Patrick, as he heard the lock slide closed on the bathroom door. He fished the coke from his suitcase and the smack from his inner left pocket, took the spoon from the back of the bottom drawer, and retrieved the half-bottle of Evian he had hidden, with unnecessary caution, behind the curtain. There might not be many more opportunities, and he'd better make a strong speed-ball to reduce the number of fixes to a minimum. He mixed the smack and coke together, dissolved them and drew the solution into the syringe.

He was ready, but how long did he have before Rachel emerged from the bathroom? With his hearing strained, like a man listening to his footsteps on a creaking staircase, he concentrated on the sounds coming from the bathroom. The muffled noise of vomiting, followed by a little rasping cough, reassured him that there would be time for a fix.

Taking no risks, he stuck the spike into a thick vein in the back of his hand. The smell of cocaine assailed him and he felt his nerves stretching like piano wires. The heroin followed in a soft rain of felt hammers playing up his spine and rumbling into his skull.

He groaned contentedly and scratched his nose. It was so pleasurable, so fucking pleasurable. How could he ever give up? It was love. It was coming home. It was Ithaca, the end of all his storm-tossed wanderings. He dropped the syringe into the top drawer, staggered across the room and sprawled on the bed.

Peace at last. The mingling lashes of half-closed eyes, the slow reluctant flutter of folding wings; his body pounded by felt hammers, pulses dancing like sand on a drum; love and poison evacuating his breath in a long slow exhalation, fading into a privacy he could never quite remember, nor for a moment forget. His thoughts shimmered like a hesitating stream, gathering into pools of discreet and vivid imagery.

He pictured his feet walking through a damp London square, his shoes sealing wet leaves darkly to the pavement. In the square, the heat from a heap of smouldering leaves syruped the air, and billows of yellow smoke skewed the sunlight like a broken wheel, its spokes scattered among the balding plane trees. The lawn was littered with dead branches, and from the railings he watched the sad and acrid ceremony, his eyes irritated by the smoke.

Patrick blinked back into the present, scratching his eye. He focused on the painting of a Normandy beach that hung above his desk. Why didn't the women in long dresses and the straw-hatted men walk into the sea? Was it the sheer gaiety of the parasols that detained them on the beach, or a sentence they must complete before disrobing their flesh in the indifferent water?

Everything was dying, every lifted stone revealed its bed of blind white maggots. He must leave the dank rotting earth and the all-consuming sea, and head for the mountains. 'I hail you, great mountains!' he chanted under his breath. 'Lofty! Alone! Serene! Good for jumping off!'

Patrick giggled feebly. The coke had already sputtered out. He was really beginning to feel rather ghastly. There was only enough for two more good fixes of coke and then he would be condemned to an accelerating agony of disappointment. The speed was perhaps only temporarily eclipsed by the heroin, but even so its performance was bound to be enormously reduced after he'd been awake for so long. The sensible thing to do in a situation like this, when one's body was a battleground strewn with the carnage of inter-narcotic wars, was to take the last Quaalude that Rachel had so high-mindedly refused, and try to have a nap on the plane. There was definitely an argument for getting some sleep; namely, that when he woke up the impact of the drugs would be stronger.

As usual, his liver ached as if he'd had a rugby ball kicked under his rib cage. His desire for drugs, like the fox hidden under the Spartan's tunic, gnawed at his entrails. The double vision which afflicted him if he didn't blink constantly had grown worse, and the two images of each object were drifting further apart.

These complaints and the general feeling that his body was held together with paper-clips and safety pins and would tear apart at the slightest strain, filled him with remorse and terror. It was always now, on the dawn of the third day, that he was filled with a disgusted desire to stop taking drugs, but he knew that the first hints of lucidity and withdrawal would bring an even greater horror of their absence.

Patrick was surprised to see Rachel standing miserably at the end of his bed. She had faded quickly from his memory while she threw up in the bathroom, losing her individuality and simply becoming Other People, someone who might interrupt his fix, or his contemplation of the rush.

'I feel so bloated,' she complained, clasping her stomach.

'Why don't you lie down?' croaked Patrick.

Rachel sank onto the bed and crawled to the far end, groaning as she collapsed on the pillows.

'Come here,' said Patrick in what he hoped was a tender voice.

Rachel rolled over slightly and lay sideways. He leant towards her, hoping she had brushed her teeth and wondering when he had last brushed his own, and kissed her. The difficult angle meant that their noses clashed and then, in their haste to overcome this awkwardness, their teeth clashed too.

'Jesus, it's like being twelve years old,' said Patrick.

'I'm sorry,' said Rachel.

He sat back with his head in one hand and ran the other hand over Rachel's knitted white dress. She looked drained and nervous. There was a bulge in her lower abdomen which had not been visible when she was standing up. Patrick skirted the bulge and brushed the back of his fingers gently over her hip and thigh.

'I'm sorry,' Rachel repeated, 'I can't go through with this, I'm too nervous. Maybe we can spend some time together, get to know each other.'

Patrick disengaged his hand and flopped back onto the bed.

'Of course,' he said flatly, glancing at the bedside clock. Four-fifty. They had about two hours and forty minutes to 'get to know each other'.

'When I was younger I used to fall into bed with anyone,' Rachel whined, 'but it always left me feeling empty.'

'Even after a plate of chili and a Banana Split?' said

Patrick, If he wasn't going to fuck her, he might as well torment her.

'You're a really hos-tel person,' said Rachel, 'do you know that? Do you have a problem with women?'

'Men, women, dogs: I don't discriminate,' said Patrick, 'they all piss me off.'

He rolled off the bed and went over to the desk. Why had he brought this tiresome lump of lard back to his room? It was intolerable, everything was intolerable.

'Look, I don't want to argue with you,' said Rachel. 'I know you're disappointed, I just need you to help me relax.'

'Relaxing isn't my speciality,' said Patrick, putting the coke and spoon into his trouser pocket and reaching to the back of the drawer to find the second syringe.

Rachel got off the bed and came over to Patrick's side.

'We're both real tired,' she said; 'let's go to bed and get some sleep. Maybe in the morning things'll seem different,' she said coyly.

'Will they?' asked Patrick. Her hand was burning into his back. He didn't want to be touched by her or by anybody else. He wriggled away, waiting for the opportunity to leave her.

'What's in this box?' asked Rachel, with a renewed effort at cheerfulness, touching the casket on top of the television.

'My father's ashes.'

'Your father's ashes.' She gulped, retracting her hand. 'That makes me feel weird.'

'I wouldn't worry about it,' said Patrick. 'I think it counts as hand luggage, don't you?'

'I guess,' said Rachel, puzzled by this line of argument. 'God, I mean, I really feel weird about this. Your father is in the room with us. Maybe I sensed that before.'

'Who knows? Anyway, he can keep you company while I'm in the bathroom. I may be some time.'

'This is heavy,' said Rachel, round-eyed.

'Don't be alarmed. He was a charming man, everybody said so.'

Patrick left Rachel in the bedroom and locked the bathroom door behind him. She sat on the edge of the bed, looking anxiously at the casket, as if she expected it to move. She took this golden opportunity to use the breathing exercises she dimly remembered from her two yoga classes, but after a couple of minutes she grew bored and still wanted to leave. The trouble was that she lived way over in Brooklyn. The cab ride was going to be ten–twelve dollars, and she would only arrive a couple of hours before she had to struggle to the gallery on the subway. If she stayed here she might get some sleep and some breakfast. She snuggled up with the breakfast menu and, after the initial excitement and guilt of seeing how many wonderful things there were to eat, she was overcome by tiredness.

Patrick lay in the bathtub, one leg dangling over the edge of the bath, blood trickling from his arm. He'd put all the coke in one last fix and, blasted by the rush, had fallen off the edge of the bath. Now he stared at the chrome shower rail and the glossy white ceiling, drawing shallow breaths through his gritted teeth, as if a girder had collapsed on his chest. Dark patches of sweat stained his shirt, and his nostrils were powdered with heroin. He had pressed the packet straight to his nose, and now it lay crumpled and empty on his neck.

With his left hand he ground the spike of the syringe against the side of the bath. He had to stop shooting up – especially now that he had run out of gear.

All the harm he'd done crowded in on him at once, like a troupe of fallen angels in a medieval painting, goading him towards hell with red-hot pitchforks, their sniggering and malicious faces surrounding him with ugliness and despair. He felt the irresistible desire to make an eternal resolution, to make the devout and impossible promise never to take a drug again. If he survived now, if he was allowed to survive, he would never shoot up again.

In this grave predicament, his fervour outweighed the knowledge of his dishonesty, even though he already detected, like distant gunfire, the disturbing feeling that something was missing. He had run out of gear. One syringe was destroyed and the other blocked with blood. It was just as well, but it was infinitely sad. Soon enough, his synapses would be screaming like starving children, and every cell in his body tugging pathetically at his sleeve.

Patrick moved his leg down tentatively and hoisted himself upright. Nearly died again. Always a shock to the system. Better take that Quaalude. He heaved himself up, nearly fainted and, leaning heavily on the wall like an old man, stepped carefully out of the bath. His coat was lying on the floor (he'd often thought of asking his tailor to put flaps in the sleeves) and he very slowly picked it up, very slowly took out the Quaalude, put it in his mouth and washed it down with a little water.

Dazed, Patrick sat down on the loo and unhooked the phone. 243–1726.

'I cannot come to the phone right now, but if you leave . . .' Fuck, he wasn't in.

'Pierre, it's Patrick. I just rang to say goodbye,' he lied. 'I'll be in touch the *moment* I get back to New York. Bye now.'

Next, he rang Johnny Hall in London to make sure there would at least be something waiting for him when he arrived. The phone rang a few times. Maybe Johnny could meet him at the airport. It rang a few more times. Jesus Christ, he wasn't in either. It was intolerable.

Patrick tried to hook the phone back, missing several times before he got it on the receiver. He was as weak as a child. Noticing that the syringe was still in the bath he picked it up wearily, wrapped it in loo

211

paper and threw it in the waste-paper basket under the basin.

In the bedroom, Patrick found Rachel stranded on the bed, snoring erratically. If he were in love, he thought. But couldn't finish. The flame play of disturbed water under a bridge's arch, a muffled echo, a kiss. Snow sliding from his boots in front of the stove, blood swelling back into his fingertips. If he were in love.

As it was, white-bellied and heavy-breathing, she looked to Patrick like a beached whale.

Packing was easy if you rolled everything into one ball, stuffed it in the suitcase, sat on it and did up the zip. He had to undo the zip again to squeeze Victor's book in. 'I think I'm an egg, therefore I am an egg,' he squealed in Pierre's French accent. Putting on his last clean shirt, he went back into the bathroom to call the reception.

'Hello?' he drawled.

'Yes, sir, how may I help you?'

'I'd like a limo at seven-thirty, please. A big one with black windows,' he added childishly.

'I'll arrange that for you, sir.'

'And prepare my bill, will you?'

'Yes, sir. Shall I send a bellboy to collect your baggage?'

'In about quarter of an hour, thank you.'

Everything was under control. He finished dressing, put on his eyepatch, and sat in the armchair waiting for the man to collect his bag. Should he leave a note for Rachel? 'I do not think I shall ever forget our evening together,' or 'Let's do this again sometime soon.' Sometimes silence was more eloquent.

There was a faint knock on the door. The bellboy was about sixty, small, bald, and dressed in the hotel's plainest grey uniform.

'There's only one bag.'

'Roight, sir,' he said in an Irish accent.

They walked down the corridor, Patrick a little stooped to protect his liver, and lopsided from the pain in his back.

'Life's not just a bag of shit,' said Patrick conversationally, 'but a leaky one. You can't help being touched by it, don't you find?'

'I believe dat's what a lot of people feel about it,' the other man replied in a lilting and agreeable tone. And then he came to a halt and put Patrick's bag down.

'And there will be rivers of blood. And de wicked shall be drowned,' he intoned. 'Nor shall de high places be spared.'

'One of your own prophecies?' asked Patrick suavely.

'It's in de Boible,' said the bellboy. 'And de bridges shall be swept away,' he promised, pointing to the ceiling and then swatting an invisible fly. 'And men shall say that de end of de world cometh upon them.'

'And they shall have a point,' said Patrick, 'but I really must be going.'

'Roight you are,' said the bellboy, still excited. 'I'll be meeting you at the reception.' He scuttled off towards the service elevator.

Try as one might to live on the edge, thought Patrick, getting into the other lift, there was no point in competing with people who believed what they saw on television.

The bill for two thousand one hundred and fifty three dollars was larger than even Patrick had expected. He was secretly pleased. Capital erosion was another way to waste his substance, to become as thin and hollow as he felt, to lighten the burden of undeserved good fortune, and commit a symbolic suicide while he still dithered about the real one. He also nursed the opposite fantasy that when he became penniless he would discover some incandescent purpose born of his need to make money. On top of the hotel bill, he must have spent another two or two and a half thousand on taxis, drugs and restaurants, plus six thousand for the air tickets. That brought the total to over ten thousand dollars, and the funeral expenses were on their way. He felt like a gameshow winner. How irritating if it had been eight and a half or nine. Ten thousand in two days. Nobody could say he didn't know how to have fun.

Patrick tossed his American Express card onto the counter without bothering to verify the bill.

'Oh, by the way,' he yawned, 'I'll sign the form, but could you leave the total open. A friend of mine is still in the room. She may want breakfast; in fact,

I'm sure she will. She can order anything she likes,' he added munificently.

'O-kay.' The receptionist hesitated, wondering whether to make an issue of the double occupancy. 'She'll be leaving the room by noon, will she?'

'I suppose so. She works, you see,' said Patrick as is this were rather exceptional. He signed the credit card form.

'We'll send a copy of the total to your home address.'

'Oh, I wouldn't bother to do that,' said Patrick, yawning again. He noticed the bellboy standing nearby with his bag. 'Hello,' he smiled. 'Rivers of blood, eh?'

The bellboy looked at him with servile incomprehension. Maybe he'd imagined the whole thing. Might be a good idea to get some sleep.

'I hope you enjoyed your stay with us,' said the receptionist, handing Patrick a copy of the bill in an envelope.

'Enjoyed isn't the word,' said Patrick with his most charming smile, 'I loved it.' He refused the envelope with a little frown. 'Oh, my God,' he suddenly exclaimed, 'I've forgotten something in the room.' He turned to the bellboy. 'There's a wooden box on top of the television; you couldn't go and fetch it for me, could you? And the brown paper bag would be very useful too.'

How could he have forgotten the box? No need to call Vienna for an interpretation. What would they

215

have done on the bleak Cornish estuary where his father had asked to have his ashes scattered? He would have had to bribe a local crematorium to give him some of their spare sweepings.

The bellboy returned ten minutes later. Patrick stubbed out his cigarette and took the brown paper bag from him. The two of them walked together towards the revolving doors.

'The young lady was wondering where you were going,' said the bellboy.

'What did you say?'

'I said I thought it was de airport.'

'And what did she say?'

'I wouldn't loik to repeat it, sir,' said the bellboy respectfully.

So much for that, thought Patrick, spinning through the doors. Slash. Burn. Move on. Out into the scintillating light, under a paler wider sky, his eyeballs drilled like a Roman statue.

Across the street he saw a man, his left arm severed at the wrist, a slight rawness where the bone was most prominent, a four days' unshaven, bitter face, yellow lenses, curling lip, lank hair, stained raincoat. The stump twitched upwards in brisk involuntary jerks. Heavy smoker. Hater of the world. *Mon semblable*. Other people's words.

Still, there were some important differences. Patrick distributed banknotes to the doorman and the bellboy. The driver opened the door for him and he climbed into the back with his brown paper bag. He sprawled across the black leather seat, closed his eyes and pretended to sleep.

A Selected List of Fiction Available from Minerva

The prices shown below were correct at the time of going to press.

☐	7493 9130 8	**The War of Don Emmanuel's Nether Parts** Louis de Bernières	£5.99
☐	7493 9962 7	**Senor Vivo and the Coca Lord** Louis de Bernières	£5.99
☐	7493 9857 4	**The Troublesome Offspring of Cardinal Guzman**	
		Louis de Bernières	£6.99
☐	7493 9720 9	**Man Kills Woman** D. L. Flusfeder	£6.99
☐	7493 9124 3	**Honour Thy Father** Lesley Glaister	£4.99
☐	7493 9960 0	**Trick or Treat** Lesley Glaister	£4.99
☐	7493 9112 X	**Hopeful Monsters** Nicholas Mosley	£6.99
☐	7493 9819 1	**Lemprière's Dictionary** Lawrence Norfolk	£6.99
☐	7493 9704 7	**Ulverton** Adam Thorpe	£5.99
☐	7493 9747 0	**Swing Hammer Swing!** Jeff Torrington	£5.99
☐	7493 9134 0	**Rebuilding Coventry** Sue Townsend	£4.99
☐	7493 9151 0	**Boating for Beginners** Jeanette Winterson	£4.99